THE WARWAGON

It was a cleverly disguised marvel of space-age technology—a rolling battleship, scout car, and base camp—outfitted with the most sophisticated electronic systems and combat capabilities. It housed the man and provided the necessary animal comforts. It kept him informed of enemy movements. It gave him mobility, cover, logistic necessities, and "big punch" capability. Its optic systems provided him with the vision of a hawk by day, an owl by night. More importantly, perhaps, the warwagon gave Mack Bolan a home.

It was designed to wage war against the Mafia . . . and, interestingly enough, it was paid for by the Mafia. In cold cash, and blood.

Now the blitz trail was leading to Canada. The warwagon would soon be delivering the Executioner's private brand of hell-on-wheels into the city of Montreal.

D0724958

The Executioner Series

the EXECUTIONER
CANADIAN CRISIS
by Don Pendleton

PINNACLE BOOKS • NEW YORK CITY

THE EXECUTIONER: CANADIAN CRISIS

Copyright © 1975 by Pinnacle Books, Inc.

All rights reserved, including the right to reproduce this book or portions thereof in any form.

An original Pinnacle Books edition, published for the first time anywhere.

ISBN: 0-523-00779-5

First printing, December 1975

Cover illustration by Gil Cohen

Printed in the United States of America

PINNACLE BOOKS, INC.
275 Madison Avenue
New York, N.Y. 10016

CONTENTS

"For every social wrong there must be a remedy. But the remedy can be nothing less than the abolition of the wrong."
—Henry George, *Social Problems*

The Mafia is cloaked in one color, black. There are no shades of gray, no shreds of white. And spilling their blood is the only sure method of eradicating the black stain of their existence.
—Mack Bolan, *The Executioner*

PROLOGUE

"Life is a competition and I am a competitor. I have the tools and the skills, and I must accept the responsiblities. I will fight the battle, spill the blood, smear myself with it, and stand at the bar of judgment to be crushed and ingested by those I serve." So declared one lone warrior as he set upon his road to hell. Mack Bolan was no crusader. He was, simply, a man doing his duty as he saw it. "To be truly alive, you have to be ready to *die* for something. Harder still, there are times when you have to be willing to *kill* for something. I am both ready to die and willing to kill."

Bolan had been "ready" throughout more than a score of campaigns against his natural enemy. He knew them, he knew their ways, and he knew the only way to stop them. "They live by the law of the jungle. It is the only law they understand and respect. And the jungle is my own place. They will find me on every trail, in every movement of the wind, in every shiver of the night. Until I die."

He had not, of course, expected to live so long. A man alone does not set himself against the most powerful crime syndicate in history and expect longevity in the bargain. He had not honestly expected to live through the first pitched battle. Nor the second, nor the third. By then, life for Mack Bolan had become an endless series of bloody battles, a war without end. Each stunning victory led only to the next battleground and another "swim through blood river."

There had been many times when he would have welcomed death, release from the commitment, final peace. But he was a stubborn sort of warrior. He was also a realist, and he knew that his war had accomplished very little in real value to the world. The enemy was as strong as ever— and, actually, becoming stronger with each passing day. Bolan had long ago given up any notion that he might actually destroy the Mafia, as he had once so boldly promised to do. Only an aroused society could write *finis* to such an all-pervading presence but, so far, most of the world seemed to be unconcerned or unaware that a monster malignancy was gnawing at their vital organs, that a determined and well-organized criminal conspiracy was laboring night and day to establish the law of the jungle to rule the affairs of the world.

Bolan could not allow himself the luxury of death. Not yet. He was fighting a delaying action, and he knew it. Men with their lofty ideals of morality and justice could not make peace with a superior force of savages; Bolan knew that. The savages sneered at lofty ideals, spat at justice, were unable to recognize morality. They understood one law, one ideal.

Yes, Mack Bolan knew his enemy.

Until the world became ready, until good men could "stay hard" against the creeping cancer of organized crime, there was but one answer to the Mafia:

I am not their judge.
I am their Judgment.
I am the Executioner.

1:   BORDER PLAY

A sleek GMC motor home wheeled silently into the parking lot of *The Natural,* a modest bistro on Buffalo's north side, and came to rest near a dimly lit rear entrance. The time was precisely midnight, the parking lot about half-filled. The amplified sounds of a western band spilled into the misty night from within the bar.

Two men appeared from the shadows at the corner of the building near the rear entrance to gaze suspiciously at the big vehicle—dark, burly men with "torpedo" patently stamped into their aggressive stance and scowling faces.

Most men would have quietly turned and walked the other way to avoid an encounter with these two in a lonely place.

Not so the occupant of that "motor home."

He descended quickly and silently, a barely discernible moving shadow of the night, and had closed half the distance to that rear door before the guardians could react to his presence there.

The reaction, when it came, was instinctive but well coordinated—quick, decisive, deadly to the ordinary interloper. Each whirled in a beautifully choreographed crouch, putting distance between each other, pistols appearing from nowhere and swinging into a quick lineup on that gliding target.

This "target" was no ordinary interloper, however. Clad in a black outfit that clung like skin, tall and graceful with a carriage that spoke of superb physical conditioning, his response was instant and final. Without a noticeable break in his forward movement, twin muzzle flashes erupted from the bulbous tip of a weapon in his right hand—silent pencils of flame performing a small arc that told the tale of death for two on the wing. It was a seemingly impersonal and uncalculated act, almost automatic in its spontaneity yet bizarre in its quietly sighing effect as the silenced weapon chugged the whispering emissaries of death into the night.

Thus died "Ponies" Latta and Harry the Hearse, two of the "meanest boys" in Buffalo—torpedo scowls intact to the end though now collapsing into the center of the red fountains of their faces, educated trigger fingers still several pounds of pull too shy—pitching simultaneously onto their backs with only gurgling sighs to mark their souls' departure.

And the man in black went on without pause, striding between the carcasses and straight to the door and through with a well-placed kick which carried him inside and along a darkened hallway to another door. He passed on by that one, going to a curtained doorway overlooking the barroom.

A bartender was rolling dice with a couple of sleepy-eyed patrons. Scantily clad cocktail waitresses roamed here and there through a listless crowd at tables. Three musicians in bright western costumes struggled to entertain indifference while a pretty kid in a G-string boredly bounced bared breasts in the background.

The waitresses and the dancer were the only females in the place.

A gleam of satisfaction stirred briefly from the icy depths of the tall man's gaze as he turned back to the mission goal. He rapped lightly on the closed door then went on in without awaiting an invitation.

Robert "Naturals" Gramelli sat at a battered wooden desk, his back to the wall. Naturals was the boss of this side of Buffalo. He was holding court with his two *caporegimes*, Ben Mazzo and Charley Cantillo. A fourth man sat nervously in the background, smiling at his clasped hands.

Only Gramelli's head swiveled to the open doorway. His jaw dropped, eyes bulging—and the final image recorded upon those horrified retinas

3

was a tall figure in black occupying that doorway, a silent flame blowing from a long black pistol extended into the room at waist level, and perhaps—in that final instant of heightened awareness—the sizzling little projectile itself which *thwacked* in between those eyes.

Mazzo and Cantillo hardly had time to appreciate the event, themselves sprawling floorward under an identical impetus. The nervous young man at the back wall smiled on, his gaze traveling from clasped hands to a brief inspection of carnage to Judgment in the doorway.

"Mack Bolan," he calmly declared, moving nothing but his lower lip.

"Your name Chebleu?" inquired the cold voice from the doorway.

"It is."

"Let's go."

"You have come for me?"

"I didn't come for them," replied the man in black, that gaze flicking briefly floorward. He tossed a military marksman's medal into the room and repeated, "Let's go."

Andre Chebleu, survivor—a ghost from the past with name and face that recalled pain and rage for the man in black—quietly got to his feet and followed the Executioner outside.

"You look like her," Bolan told him.

"With you, I will probably end like her," the Canadian replied.

"Either way," Bolan said, sighing. "Your cover

4

is blown here. They were setting you up for the kill. Tonight."

"How do you know this?"

Bolan directed Georgette Chebleu's brother to the warwagon and told him, "I'll show you. Then you're going to show me something, brother Andy."

That soft smile passed without a quiver over the crumpled remains of the outside guards as Chebleu hurried to the vehicle.

"What could *I* show *you?*" he asked quietly.

"The other side."

The undercover operative from Canada stepped into the motor home with a quizzical smile playing at the worried eyes. "The other side of what?"

"The other side of hell," Bolan told him. "That's where we're headed."

"Right now?"

"Right now," said the Executioner.

2: THE SIDES

The "warwagon" was a cleverly disguised marvel of space-age technology—a rolling battleship, scout car, and base camp—outfitted with the most sophisticated electronic systems and combat capabilities. It housed the man and provided the necessary animal comforts. It kept him informed of enemy movements and even their plots and schemes. It gave him mobility, cover, logistic necessities, and "big punch" capability. More importantly, perhaps, the warwagon gave Mack Bolan a home—and the home certainly fit the man.

Her optic systems provided him with the vision of a hawk by day, an owl by night—even the "sight" of a bat in zero-visibility conditions. In open country, her audio scanners could detect a sniffle at a thousand yards; radio scanners covered the entire UHF/VHF spectrum to provide constant monitoring of combat-zone radio communications—including police radio. Her "surveillance" console had the capability to automatically "trigger" remote listening devices to collect, record, sort, and store intelligence data at millisecond speeds.

Bolan was justly proud of his combat vehicle.

He did not disclose all her secrets to Andre Chebleu but he did "show" the man how he had tumbled to the intrigue in Buffalo, then sat him down to read the intelligence file gathered in that area.

While Chebleu studied the file, Bolan pulled dungarees and a flannel shirt over the combat suit, donned an old fishing hat, and sent the warwagon powering north along the Interstate toward Niagara Falls.

At Tonawanda, Chebleu came forward to drop into the seat opposite the command chair. He gazed thoughtfully at the stoic profile of his host and said, with a soft sigh, "Amazing."

"What is?" Bolan asked, his gaze remaining on the road ahead.

"All of it. You. This fantastic vehicle. The file. All I was sent here to learn, you possess in that file. I have been here for three months. How long have you?"

Bolan grinned. "Three days. I didn't design the gear, Andre. I simply use it. You guys could use the same thing."

The Canadian spread his hands and made a wry face. "It is against the law."

"So am I," Bolan said quietly.

"Yes. So you are. And I *am* the law. So what does that make *us?*"

"Soldiers of the same side," Bolan replied. "As long as you want it that way."

"And suppose I want it differently? When we cross the border?"

Bolan shrugged. "Then you go your way and I go mine. I didn't kidnap you, guy. I sprung you. Say the word. I'll stop and let you out."

Chebleu lit a cigarette and relaxed into the seat, turning his gaze onto the roadway. They drove in silence, the powerful engine pulling the big rig effortlessly along just under the speed limit. The traffic was heavy but moving nicely. Now and then a speeding vehicle would surge past them, Chebleu stiffening with each such instance. The full implications of the night were obviously just beginning to settle onto the guy. After some miles of this, he told Bolan: "Perhaps I owe you my life. Thank you."

The guy did not like him, though, and Bolan knew it. He fished the AutoMag from its special pocket in the command chair and handed the big silver pistol to his guest. "Thumb off the safety," he growled. "Now put the snout to my ear."

The Canadian merely stared at him.

Bolan chuckled and held out his hand. "Give it

back, then," he said. "Now I owe you my life. We're even."

Chebleu laughed faintly as he returned the pistol. "How did you know I would not?"

"I didn't know," Bolan assured him. "Now I do."

Both laughed, together, and Chebleu offered his rescuer a cigarette. Bolan accepted it, took a deep drag, then said, "We're not quite even yet, Chebleu. I think you know what I mean."

"Georgette," the guy replied immediately.

"Yeah. Were you given the details?"

Georgette's brother shook his head solemnly. "Just an unofficial communiqué from your government, expressing sympathy and confirming her death. I have not yet fully accepted—I keep hoping . . ."

"Stop hoping," Bolan said quietly.

"Until there is a body, I will not—" Something in Bolan's tone produced a delayed reaction, shutting the guy down in mid-sentence. He dropped his eyes and said, "Tell me."

"Just take my word." The voice was taut, saddened, sympathetic all at once. "Georgette is dead. She lived large and she died large. Now bury her that way."

"Tell me," the guy insisted.

Bolan sighed, eased off to the minimum speed, and told the guy. "Crazy Sal sentenced her to fifty days in a turkey doctor's chamber of horrors."

9

"What?" Chebleu croaked.

"You know what a turkey doctor is?"

The guy was shaking his head, obviously hoping that he did not know.

Bolan said, "Think of Auschwitz, Buchenwald, and the madmen who played medical games there with human meat. Then think of that sort of mentality transplanted to this time and place, give it the absolute power that is enjoyed by a mob boss, and turn it loose on a cute kid who got too cute with that same boss. You can forget names and identities now, because there's nothing left but screaming turkey. It must have been about the forty-ninth day when I found Georgette."

The guy turned very pale, covering his eyes with a hand, fighting for control over his emotions.

Quietly, Bolan said, "I released her, Andre. With that same weapon you were just holding. I put a 240-grain bullet where her eyes had been. And her soul thanked mine. Bury her, guy. Bury her very, very large."

It was several quiet minutes later when Chebleu lit another cigarette. He handed it to Bolan and lit another for himself. The voice, when it came, was rock hard. "This was in Detroit?"

"Yeah. On the back porch of hell."

"Thank you for telling me."

"You had a right to know," Bolan said.

"So now I know. You left very little in Detroit."

"I took what I could."

"So, now . . . Canada is next."

Bolan sighed. "That's right. And if you studied that file closely, then you know . . ."

Yes, Chebleu knew. The entire province of Quebec had suddenly gone up for grabs. A governmental crisis was brewing up there—a national convulsion being fed by separatist politics, economic woes, fierce nationalism, the spirit of open rebellion. Beneath that cauldron the American Mafia was now building a bonfire. Bolan had been aware of the situation for some time, and had been quietly probing the American side for a likely angle of entry. Andre Chebleu had come as a gift from heaven.

"The mob is getting ready to eat Quebec," Bolan told him.

The guy grunted at that, then added, "They will find it indigestible."

"Chewed is chewed," Bolan pointed out. "They don't want your problems, friend. They just want your juices."

"Your heart does not beat for Canada," the guy said, eyeing his host with a trace of displeasure. "If you seek only a battlefield, seek it elsewhere."

Bolan checked his rearview, signaled, slowed, and pulled off the road onto the shoulder. He opened the door from the master control and told his guest, "Good-bye. Stay hard."

"You will need help," the guy said, grimacing with some inner emotion.

"I'll find it where I need it," Bolan told him.

"Close the door," Chebleu growled. "What is your plan?"

"Very simple," Bolan replied, as he resumed the vehicle's forward motion. "I'll be blitzing Montreal."

"You will find that not so simple."

"It never is," Bolan said.

"You cannot blitz Montreal," Chebleu insisted.

Bolan shot the guy an oblique glance and told him, "Sit there and watch me try."

"Montreal will prove to be Detroit times one hundred for you."

"For them," Bolan corrected him.

"For you as well, my friend," the Canadian said, sighing. "For you as well."

"The question may be academic, anyway," Bolan replied, his attention at the rearview mirror. "We have a tail."

Chebleu slowly shifted his gaze rearward. "You are positive?"

"I'm positive. They have one headlamp just slightly off focus. See it?"

"I see it."

"Been with us since we left Naturals'. When I pulled over, just now, those lights suddenly disappeared. Now they're back."

Bolan was busy with the command console. He swung out a small viewscreen and activated the

Nitebrite Optics. The screen glowed with a dull reddish light. Bolan adjusted the azimuth control and refined the focus. A vehicle appeared there, in close-up—a heavy limousine, heavily loaded, cruising the warwagon's backtrack.

"Bingo," Bolan said quietly. "It's a crew wagon."

The Canadian agent's nervousness was returning.

"You knew that when you ordered me outside," he declared accusingly.

"I wouldn't have let you go," Bolan said with a small smile.

"So what do we do now?"

"They're tracking us into a hit," Bolan told him. "Just waiting for a stretch of empty road."

"So?"

"So we wait them out. And we'll play their game—but our way."

"I'll take that pistol, now," Chebleu said.

"Not this one. Go aft." Bolan punched a button on the console. "Armory's open. Choose your weapon."

Chebleu was smiling grimly. "So. You knew it all the while."

"Suspected," Bolan corrected. "For better or for worse—it's you and me, Andre, soldiers together."

"Of the same side," the Canadian growled, and went aft for his weapon.

3: ENGAGEMENT AT NIAGARA

Tommy Sandini and his Broadway crew were just pulling into the front lot at Naturals' as the big RV was easing out the other end. One of the boys even made a joke about Gramelli's business "picking up by the busload."

Sandini himself had not even stepped out of the car before one of his boys discovered the dead bodies near the back entrance to the club. A quick look inside confirmed the awful suspicions, and a fast calculation of two plus two sent the Sandini crew highballing after that "bus."

"Those bodies were still warm, boss," reported tagman Vacchi.

"Still bleeding, he means," added another.

"Everybody back inside!" Tough Tommy commanded. "Which way'd that bus go?"

"Went up Delaware," the wheelman muttered. "Everybody just hang on, I'll be up their ass in two snorts."

And thus the chase began.

As it turned out, more than a couple of snorts were required before wheelman Roselli could close the distance between the two vehicles. By that time, the chase had turned east along Sheridan Drive.

"They're headed for the Thruway," Sandini growled. "Lay back and let 'em go, let's see where it takes us."

"We could hit 'em at Sheridan Park," Vacchi suggested.

"Hit, hit, *what* hit?" the boss snarled. "We don't even know who it is. Maybe we ought to be back at Gramelli's, taking that joint apart."

"I got an idea, Tommy," the wheelman said. "That bus ain't no bus. Know what it is?"

Sandini respected his wheelman, especially in anything concerning automobiles. He growled, "It's one of those camper things, isn't it?"

"Right, an RV, so-called recreational vehicle. That one up there is pretty jazzy but it's still an RV. You know what I heard from a guy was out in Seattle awhile back—you know when? When the fur was flying out there."

"You mean the Bolan thing."

"Yeah. This guy says Hardcock Bolan was driving one of them things, an RV."

"Shit," Sandini responded, in a sibilant whisper.

"That's what the guy said, Tommy."

"Let's uh, keep a distance. If uh, if what you say ..." The boss's mouth got lost in his mind, and a strained silence descended upon that group.

Presently one of the young hardmen who had discovered the bodies of Gramelli and lieutenants inside the club made a strange sound and touched his boss's shoulder from the jump seat.

"What is it?" Sandini asked in a subdued voice.

"I picked something up back there. Had blood on it. I just wiped it off and dropped it in my pocket. Didn't really hit me, boss."

"*What* didn't?"

"What does a marksman's medal look like?"

"It's a bull's-eye cross," Vacchi said quickly.

"Oh shit," said the young gunner. "I thought it was a religious medal."

"Let me see that thing!" Sandini demanded, reaching for it.

A moment later, it all came together—and the Sandini crew from the Broadway territory knew they had a tiger by the tail.

"What're we going to do?" Vacchi mildly inquired of his boss.

"We're going to stay on his ass, that's what we're going to do," Sandini snarled back. "Now shut up and let me think about it."

The wheelman quietly got in his favorite gripe.

"We should've gone radio-equipped, Tommy, like I been saying. We could get some help out here."

"Shut up!"

"Sure, Tommy."

It was a whisper from one of the youngsters in the rear, but it came through loud and clear. "Shit, there's six of us. We could take 'im."

"How many was back there at Naturals'?" Vacchi purred.

"That was different," replied the anonymous whisper. "He caught them cold. This is diferent."

"Shut up that fuckin' whispering back there!" Sandini howled. "What is this? A goddamn hunt club? Shut up back there! That's a million-dollar baby up there, not no goddamn pigeon tied to a stake!"

"There's our last chance," the wheelman reported. "He's taking the Thruway uh—yeah, yeah, north ramp. We're headed north."

"Stay with him!"

"You wanta drop a boy off, boss, before it's too late? Get to a phone, I mean."

"Fuck no, forget that! Okay, yeah! Fonti—get out! Call Joe Staccio! Tell 'im what we got here and to goddammit get us some help up here. Get a damn helicopter, get anything, just get some help and quick!"

"Headed toward Niagara?" the kid grunted as he tumbled through the doorway.

"Just tell 'im what you know!" Sandini yelled —and again they were off.

"So what do we do?" Vacchi asked the boss.

"We keep back and give him room to run, that's what. Not too close, dammit—just run him."

"This traffic is pretty thick," the wheelman reported. "I better not give him too much slack."

"The guy might be headed for the Ontario side," Vacchi worried. "We ought to hit him before that."

"There's plenty of spots between here and there," said Roselli.

"I'll tell you when," Sandini growled. "Let's give Joe Staccio all the time we can to spring some help this way."

"I know a perfect spot," Roselli muttered. "This time of night—if he takes Mose Parkway into the Falls . . . that's a perfect spot, boss."

"I'll tell you when," Sandini fretted. It was perhaps the largest moment of his life. He was not about to blow it. "You boys listen to me. This is the big one, the mother lode. We get Mack Bolan's head in a sack and we can write our own ticket anywhere. You understand me? This is the *big* one."

The pep talk was unnecessary. Each man in that fated vehicle knew very well the size of this moment. Riches, reputation, rank, glory—all was represented in that dim glow of taillights running the road to Niagara Falls. And five glazed gazes knew it. The Sandini crew was ready to fulfill its destiny.

18

They rolled over Buckhorn Island and across the Niagara River, then west along the river route. Chebleu told Bolan, "This is the zone I would choose for the attack."

"I expected them sooner than this," Bolan replied. He did not like the cat-and-mouse aspect which had developed here. "They're playing it too cozy. Must be expecting reinforcements somewhere along the way. Get ready, Andre. We start our game now."

Chebleu nodded and took his position—on the floor, at the midships doorway—a light autopistol at the ready.

They were moving along within a small clump of traffic, flowing leisurely at the speed limit— perhaps a dozen vehicles, in all—the tail car hanging grimly to the trailing edge of the formation.

Bolan hit his flasher and the wheel at the same instant, tromping the accelerator and swinging into a gap in the adjacent traffic lane, gathering momentum and weaving through the pack until he was clear and hurtling along in a free run toward the next pack, far ahead.

The crew vehicle, though faster and more maneuverable, was not finding the holes quite so well. The warwagon was a full thousand meters out front before the other car broke clear—but then the gap began quickly shortening between the two, and Bolan knew that it was going to be a horse race into the chosen zone of combat. He needed a lonely stretch, a place where innocent bystanders would not be subjected to the hellfire of open warfare. And that place lay just ahead. The countdown was on. The engagement at Niagara was about to be consummated.

"Did you *see* that!" Sandini cried. "He's sniffed us! He's running!"

"Not far," Roselli growled, leaning toward a hole to the right.

From the jump seat, Vacchi marveled, "I didn't know those big jobs could move that fast."

Roselli swore and tromped his brake. That hole on the right had disappeared. He hit his horn and surged up to the rear bumper of the car ahead. The guy up there was watching him through the rearview but otherwise ignoring that presence on his tailgate.

Sandini yelled, "Move 'im, dammit! We're losing the show!"

It was at such times that a professional wheelman earned his daily bread. Roselli growled, "We're going through—hang on." The big car leapt onto the bumper of the car ahead—just a tap and a shove before falling back and swerving right to graze the other vehicle of the box.

The startled drivers of the other cars immediately gave room, the one falling back and the other surging ahead. Roselli cackled as he swung into the hole and he flipped a finger at the driver on his left as he powered on through and ahead.

The lights of the "bus" were receding into the distance as he extricated himself from the rest of the pack and began really laying rubber.

"Move it, move it," Sandini growled.

"We're doing a flat hundred."

"Don't give me speed reports, dammit. *Catch that bastard!*"

"He ain't going nowhere, boss."

"Damn right he ain't. We take no more chances." Sandini swiveled tautly toward the rear. "You boys get it ready. Shoot the son of a bitch off the road. Rosy will tell you when. Right, Rosy?"

"Right," the wheelman replied. He was hunched over the wheel, giving the big cruiser every rein she would take. "I'll pull by fast," he explained. "Get your windows down, back there. Hoss—you lay your shotgun right down in the tit of the window. I'll put you right even with the driver's seat. That's when you let go, and that's when I let go. We're going to be moving like hell, so don't muff it."

"We gotta stay clear," Sandini cautioned. "Don't want the damn thing rolling over on us."

"You blow 'im away with that shotgun, Hoss," Roselli said. "I'll take care of the rest, boss."

The Broadway crew trusted wheelman Roselli's instincts in a moving vehicle. There was no real worry in that regard. It was Vacchi who voiced the real worry. "Sounds too easy," he fretted. "That guy isn't going to let us just slide up there

21

and start booming away. If he's sniffed us, then he's getting ready for us. That's for sure."

"You got a better plan?" Sandini asked coldly.

"No, I guess not."

"Hit 'im, Rosy. Just like you called it."

They were moving up, now, swiftly and surely, eating away the distance to sudden riches and glory. The RV was no more than a football field ahead.

Sandini suddenly made a noise in his throat, following with: "Do you see that?"

"What, boss?"

"I thought that bus was flat on top. Now it's got a—a . . ."

"Air conditioner," Roselli said, instinctively slowing the advance, however.

"Naw, naw, that ain't what that is," Sandini growled.

Vacchi suddenly grabbed the seat by Sandini's shoulder and gasped. The "thing" above the RV was moving, swiveling about, and it suddenly became quite apparent to the ex-GI what that "thing" was. *Stop, Rosy!* he yelled. *Stop the car!*"

"You crazy?" Sandini snarled.

"It's a rocket launcher! That's a Goddamn—!"

Yes, the Broadway crew had themselves a tiger by the tail, and now all knew it for once and all—"all" being the final fleeting seconds of the motley assortment of misspent lives.

Vacchi was still trying to scream an explanation of what the "thing" was when a flaming arrow leapt clear up there and whizzed along the backtrack in a hustling intercept. The moment became frozen, illumined by the certain knowledge of what was coming for them, the horror heightened by the rustling sound the thing was making and the inevitability of the firetrack.

The big rocket met that speeding vehicle smack on the windshield, and engulfed it in a shattering, roaring, all-consuming fireball that lifted it completely off the road, spun it drunkenly in a plunging cartwheel, and swept it into the Niagara River.

And far ahead, Mack Bolan deactivated his fire-control system, retracted his launcher into the roof, and told his passenger, "Stay alert. There could be more."

Chebleu was shaken, stunned by the unexpected turn of events. "I think not," he replied quietly. "If so, they would have lost the heart, just now."

He came forward, ruefuelly inspecting his unused weapon, and dropped into the seat opposite Bolan. The look he was giving the man held new respect. "I think, also," he added quietly, "that I can hardly wait for Montreal."

Nor, indeed, could the Executioner. The French-speaking capital of North America was next on his hit parade.

4:   FROM THE TOP

Joe Staccio, as boss of the upstate New York territories, was one of the eleven iron old men who ruled the farflung *Cosa Nostra* empire. His seat on *La Commissione* had been secure and unchallenged for many years and it was generally known that his voice at the ruling council was a respected and influential one. Still, Joe Staccio knew his place. There was but one "boss of all the bosses"—and that one was Augie Marinello, the crusty old patriarch of the "five-family" New York City territory.

Augie was getting pretty old, sure, and he'd never been the same since that brush with death at the hands of one Mack Bolan in New Jersey one terrible night. He'd lost both legs to Bolan's fireworks, and his claim on life itself had been nip and tuck for a while there—but a man such as Augie Marinello did not need legs to sit at the head of the table, and he did not need the steel grip of youth to hold the reins of this savage empire. A flash of the eyes, a toss of the head, a clearing of the throat, the clenching of a feebled fist—any of these was sufficient to topple governments or ruin powerful corporations anyplace on the globe. Augie was still the boss's boss—and none had ever thought of it any other way. Particularly not Joe Staccio.

He came in quietly and kissed the old man's ring, then sat down and waited for an acknowledgment of his presence there.

Augie looked terrible. The years were piling up on him. The hair had gone snow white almost overnight, the skin on face and hands almost corrugated with wrinkles. When those eyes came open, however, the boss was still the boss.

"How you doing, Joe?" he asked tiredly.

"I'm doing fine, Augie. You're looking swell."

"I'm looking terrible and you know it," Marinello said, sighing. "I'd like to get this thing sewed up before I die."

Staccio shifted uncomfortably as he replied, "You're not going to die, Augie."

"Sure I am. Everybody dies. I'm running out of time, Joe. I know it in my bones. I want this thing sewed up, and quick."

"That's what I came to talk about."

"I know. Did you set it up?"

Staccio fidgeted some more. "The meet is set, yeah. We got an army up there to keep things in hand, and all the delegations but Greece have checked in."

"*All* of 'em?"

"Like I said, all but Greece. They're due in tonight."

"Turkey?"

"Sure, them too. That's like a little NATO we got going up there, Augie. I wish you could make it yourself."

"Something's on your mind, Joe. What is it?"

"Well . . . there could be a hitch, Augie."

"What hitch?"

"I got this wild call from Buffalo last night. One of the downtown kids. He says somebody walked in and knocked over a suburb office. About midnight. Maybe you don't remember Bobby Gramelli."

"Sure I do," the old man replied immediately. "I made Bobby more'n twenty years ago, gave 'im a numbers concession in the Bronx. What about 'im?"

"He got shot in the head last night, Augie. And four of his boys along with him. This kid that called me is from the downtown office. You know Tommy Sandini?"

Marinello shook his head. "Maybe if I saw him."

"Come to me by way of Boston, had blood connections there but he was a little wild. His uncle,

26

Charlie Sandini, asked me to take him under my wing for a while, get the kid's feet planted good. Been with me ever since. I put him in charge of the downtown Buffalo office a couple of years ago. Well Tommy Sandini and his crew happened along right as the suburb office was getting knocked over. They see this guy hottin' it out of there in one of these, uh, you know, what they call mobile home, uh, no, I mean motor home—you know, these damn trucks with a house built on them. They chased after the guy, finds him heading out the river parkway toward Niagara Falls. Well by now they've got the idea that this boy they're chasing is none other than Mack Bolan."

The old eyes flashed. "Where'd they get that?"

"One of the kids has picked up a marksman's medal, back at the suburb office. It's laying on Bobby Gramelli's dead body. This is a green kid and he don't think to mention it until the chase is on. So anyway, they drop this kid off somewheres to sound the alarm and off they go on Mack Bolan's tail. They—"

"When do you get this, Joe?"

"Right away. I'm in Syracuse, just for overnight to rest up for all that diplomatic crap in Montreal, and I get this hot call from my office in Rochester. Matty Howell there tells me this hysterical kid is on the horn with this wild story about chasing Mack Bolan out of Buffalo. I say okay and Matty switches the call over, and I get

27

it straight from the Buffalo kid. He says the chase is running toward Niagara and what should they do? I was fit to—"

The old man interrupted with a kindly comment. "This Bolan guy puts the shivers in the best boys, Joe. No need to apologize for yours."

"I know. I know, Augie. Well, anyway, I got Matty back on the horn and sent a dozen heavy crews over there. We even put a couple of helicopters in the air from Niagara and Buffalo."

"Too late."

"Sure, too late. The chopper from Niagara got there in time to see the downtown office get pulled out of the Niagara River. Their car was blown all to hell, and I guess they're still trying to piece the bodies together."

Marinello sighed and reached for a cigar. "That's the, uh, hitch you was tellin' about," he said softly.

"Yeah. I have to buy it as Mack Bolan. It's got his prints all over it. And I don't like the territory he's in, Augie. He's mighty close."

"Could be a coincidence," the old boss decided.

"Well, there's more."

Marinello was lighting his cigar. He peered out through the smoke and said, "Let's have it."

"There was a man down from Montreal, working the *Quebeçois* angle with Bobby Gramelli. Bobby had the hardware concession for the meet—I mean, from my territory. This Montreal guy is supposed to be in with the *Quebeçois* militants, see. Well—I get it this morning that this guy—he was going by the name of LeBlanc—is really working with the Canadian cops. Bobby had tumbled to that, and he was getting ready to correct his mistake. The last anybody saw of Bobby Gramelli—alive, I mean, this guy LeBlanc is under his wing. This is just a few minutes before Bobby is laying dead on his office floor. Well, Augie, this LeBlanc is nowhere around, suddenly. It looks like maybe he left with Bolan."

Marinello bit through his cigar. "I guess we got a hitch," he said quietly.

"I'm afraid so, Augie," Staccio replied worriedly.

"What've you been doing about it?"

"I got an army out looking for him. Planes and everything. He's probably already ditched that whatchacallit, motor home—but that's all we got to go on. Lot of territory to cover, Augie. If he's headed for that meet in Montreal, he could be taking a hundred different routes. The Niagara thing could mean something or maybe not. He's tricky. Shows his nose at the door to Ontario then maybe scoots for the other side. Anyway, it's hard to cover all the possibilities but I'm trying. I got crews swarming down from Montreal, covering all the routes into town for a hundred miles out. I got planes in the air and people at the airports. I even got a watch on the damn St. Lawrence Seaway. The boy is tricky, mighty tricky."

"You better go now, Joe," Marinello said tiredly. "Take personal charge of that. Don't let that guy get into Montreal."

"You got my word on that, Augie." The upstate boss rose to leave. "Don't let this bother you. I'll take care of Bolan."

"People been telling me that for a long time, Joe," the old man said.

"His luck can't run forever," Staccio said.

"You better count on something more than luck." Marinello grasped the blankets where his legs had once been. "Take that from one who knows, Joe."

"Yeah, Augie."

"If you can, bring him here. Alive."

Staccio grinned. "I'll even put a ribbon in his hair for you."

"I'd like to get that boy, alive and looking at me, knowing what he's gonna get."

"I'll bring him to you, Augie. I swear I will."

"Not like London, Joe."

The Staccio smile faded. That had been a low blow, to remind him of the fiasco in England. "I said I'd bring him, Augie. That's my personal word."

He went out of that august presence, repeating silently to himself the promise hastily made but oh so damned difficult to fulfill.

A crisis was forming in Joe Staccio's worried mind. A personal crisis, a family crisis—a crisis of the spirit. Too much was at stake at Montreal.

The world—the whole damn world—was at stake.

Joe Staccio was not going to allow one hotshot bastard to turn all that around.

"I'm gonna get his ass, Augie," he muttered as he let himself outside.

5: ON TRACK

Bolan did not underestimate the enemy. He knew that they would be watching every trail and kicking every rock in a determined effort to keep the Executioner out of Montreal.

Very important things were about to happen in that city.

An international underground congress was being convened there, with delegations attending from every area of the globe. The long whispered-about, meticulously planned, superevent of the criminal world was actually becoming a fact. The Montreal Conference was designed to give birth to *Cosa di tutti Cosi*—the Thing of all the Things—the most formidable crime cartel ever envisioned by the mind of men.

It was actually happening—and it was happening in Montreal. The American Mafia would be the nucleus of the new, formal, supercombination. Augie Marinello would be officially proclaimed *Capo di tutti Capi*—Boss of all the Bosses. His throne would be installed in the Canadian province of Quebec; Montreal would thenceforward be the crime capital of the world.

It was not a maniacal plan but a coldly calculated, heavily financed, and carefully instrumented conspiracy to seize the world.

Bolan had only a hazy understanding of the political situation in Quebec—but it was obvious that it was this situation which prompted the Mafia bosses to select Montreal as their new capital. Quebec had been a French state since Cartier landed there in the year 1534, claiming the new territory for France. It was not until 1763 that Quebec was ceded to the British, becoming the "province of Quebec," and the transformation from French to British control had never occurred in any meaningful sense.

Quebec now had two "official languages"— French and English. Schools were strictly parochial—French Catholic and English Protestant—the major emphasis on Catholicism, naturally, with a heavy majority of French Canadians in the population.

French nationalist sentiment in the province had been growing for decades and escalating into feverish intensity over the past few years. *Parti Quebeçois,* the political center of French nationalist sentiment, though still a minority party, had swollen its membership to a point where serious challenges were being made to the ruling liberals. A steadily growing sentiment within the *Quebeçois* was toward secession from the Dominion of Canada and the establishment of Quebec as a separate nation. Adding to the political unrest was the constant threat of militant action, with the young lions of the separatist movement arming and preparing for the final convulsion.

Apparently the Mob—never to be accused of failure to respond to a golden opportunity—had read something of comfort to their plans in the political atmosphere of Quebec.

Bolan's intelligence was not that complete; he did not know the specifics of Mob involvement in Canadian politics or *Quebeçois* nationalism. One thing was certain, however: whatever was happening in Canada was definitely being exploited by the men with the golden fingers—and they were about to slip Quebec into their hip pockets.

So, no, Mack Bolan did not underestimate the enemy. They would go to any lengths to write insurance for this Montreal Meet. They would not want the likes of Mack Bolan crashing their party.

With this in mind, his route to Montreal was calculated not primarily for rapid transit but toward certainty of arrival. He had gone west from Niagara Falls, into Ontario and through Hamilton to Toronto, leaving the lakeshore behind at Newcastle to angle into the interior. He reached the outskirts of Ottawa for breakfast, shared hastily with his tense friend from Montreal, then bore north for a circuitous approach to the combat zone. A normal two-hour journey from Ottawa to Montreal, Bolan took it in five—meandering through the back country in a wary advance upon his goal.

He had not deluded himself that he would reach Montreal without incident. The city is situated on an island, the St. Lawrence flowing by to the east, Rivière des Mille Isles to the west—Rivière des Prairies, also, cutting across the western suburbs. Rivers mean bridges and—bridges, to a hunted man, mean trouble.

It was midday when the warwagon nosed into a small fishing camp near Bois des Filion, at the northwest approach to the city. Bolan rented a space for his vehicle, taking the weekly rate, and two enthusiastic "fishermen" immediately went down to test the action at water's edge.

Bolan's "fishing rod" was actually a highly refined optic instrument. He patiently scanned both sides of the river, the bridge area, the skies above—then told his partner, "They're here, all right. In force."

"Then they are everywhere," Chebleu assured him.

Sure. They would be everywhere. With unlimited manpower and the riches of the world at stake—why not?

Bolan said, "I guess that Buffalo crew was expecting reinforcements at that. They got the word out, anyway." He sighed. "Well—it just makes the job harder—not impossible."

Chebleu delicately cleared his throat but said bluntly, "It is your own fault. This bravura habit of leaving behind the death medals—it is foolish. It is like a trail, a track."

"It's also a signature," Bolan replied absently, his mind obviously busy with more important matters. He grinned suddenly and said, "Bravura, eh? Well, maybe so. The psychological war is as important as any, brother Andy. My enemy understand bravura. They respect it. So maybe I lose a little by signing my hits. But it gains me a lot in the psychological war."

"Perhaps," Chebleu quietly agreed, eyeing his companion with a level gaze. The gaze fell abruptly as he asked, "Did you know that it was I who sent Georgette to her death?"

Bolan murmured, "Bury her."

"This is my way. Allow me."

"Go," Bolan replied, resigned to it.

"It was my recommendation that she be asked to take the assignment. It was a terrible crime we were investigating—a crime against the soul, you understand. So many young girls being sent into that hell, such a shocking . . . Well. One does not find reliable female operatives on any street corner. Georgette had the experience." His eyes flared. "She had the body expertise of a court-

36

esan, the mind of a great detective, the will and courage of a warrior. That she was also my own sister, I did not consider. I was simply seeking the best, and the best was Georgette. Washington readily agreed to make her available. And I used her. Like a piece of meat on a hook. I sent her into that—that . . ."

"Georgette sent herself," Bolan said coldly. "You're trying to bury yourself, not her. You'll do it, too, if you keep this up. It's a hard world, Andre. *Stay* hard, dammit."

"Stay hard," the Canadian echoed. The gaze came up, slowly. "This is the meaning of that phrase? The world is hard, so we must all, each of us, become also hard? Will the world, therefore, ever become soft?"

Bolan was again sighting through the fishing rod. "There are many worlds," he murmured. "Fish worlds, rabbit worlds, bird worlds. Are any of them soft?"

"Perhaps," Chebleu replied, shrugging. "Depending upon the point of view."

"Try one of these views," Bolan grunted. "A fish view, from the belly of a whale. A rabbit view, from a coyote's belly. A bird's view, from the talons of a hawk. Where's the soft, brother Andy?"

"That does not make it right."

Bolan's eyes flashed from the telescope. "It makes it *real*. Face this world, Andre—look at it squarely. It's divided between the eaten and the eaters. Now maybe that's not right, but dammit it's the way it is. If it makes you feel better to shake your fist at the heavens, then go ahead. I'd rather shake mine at the eaters. Stay hard? Damn right, if you intend to do anything about the situation. Can one rabbit help another out of the coyote's jaws? Georgette was no rabbit—and she was not a piece of meat on a hook. Try taking what she was away from her, brother Andy, and you also take away everything she accomplished in this life. Salute her, dammit—commend her soul to a happier place—and then, once and for all, *bury* her."

Bolan spun on his toe and returned to his battle cruiser. Chebleu returned a moment later, a faint smile playing at his lips.

"Thank you," he said softly.

Bolan tossed him a change of clothes. "Get into these," he instructed. "We're going fishing."

"From the whale's belly?"

"Maybe," Bolan replied, smiling back at his new friend.

Less than an hour later, he was stepping ashore on the east bank of Rivière des Mille Isles at a carefully selected spot. From this point, he would be on his own. Chebleu would return the boat to the fish camp and enter the city later, under his own arrangements. The warwagon was remaining at Bois des Filion, for the time being.

Chebleu shook his hand and told him, "Stay hard, *L'Exécuteur*."

Bolan smiled, said, "See you tonight," and tracked on in his penetration of the new underground capital of the world, the quiet side of his mind reflecting upon that earlier conversation with Georgette's brother. Montreal, sure, was going to be some kind of unholy bitch. It would take more than "hard" to see him through this one. He smiled, recalling Chebleu's use of the word "bravura." It meant a brilliant or daring performance.

Yeah.

It would take a hell of a lot more than that, too.

6:   BRAVURA

He stripped off the woodsy outfit and abandoned it in a clump of bushes. Over the blacksuit, then, he donned dress shirt and slacks, tie, the Beretta shoulder rig, light jacket. The empty tackle box went into the bushes with the other clothing after yielding up the final items of the transformation—a cosmetic case and dark glasses, ID wallet, monogrammed handkerchief bearing the initials FR, a few pieces of junk jewelry, also monogrammed, and initialed cigarette lighter.

From the cosmetic case he selected neatly flared long sideburns, considered and rejected brown-tinted contact lenses, then threw the case into the bushes with the other stuff.

Time consumed: about a minute.

He lit a tipped cigarette, stuck it to the side of his mouth, and took off toward the bridge at a leisurely pace.

About halfway there, a tough-looking guy with New York written all over him came hurrying around a bend in the trail. They almost collided head-on. The guy jumped back with an alarmed snarl, a .45 combat Colt there and ready.

Bolan beat him to the challenge. "What the hell're you doing down here?" he growled in his best street voice.

The enemy's greatest weakness lay in their size and secrecy. Inter-family cooperative efforts, such as the Canadian operation, was a blending of strangers groping in the dark with often little more than instincts to guide them. Bolan had often played to this weakness. He had, indeed, become a master at the game.

The guy was giving him a quick sizing as he replied, "Didn't know you were back here, man. Could've taken your damn head off. Why don't you—"

"I asked, what are you doing here?" Bolan said, cutting in coldly on the lukewarm speech.

The guy was taken somewhat aback by the ice in that voice. He was reappraising as he backpedaled a bit. "We, uh, saw a boat crossing the river—couple of guys fishing, looked like. Disappeared around the bend there. Only one guy when it came back. Larry said I should check it out."

"Larry was right," the iceman said. He grinned suddenly, allowing a slight thaw as he added, "But it was just me." He took the guy by the arm and turned him around. "Come on, we're pulling out."

The guy's mind was tumbling, trying to pull things together. "I don't, uh, he didn't say ..."

Through it all, Bolan's confiding tone was mildly complaining: "Been in that damn fish camp over there since two this morning. Ridiculous! Frank Ruggi don't sit around half a day in the woods, cracking his knuckles. Dumb! I called Augie and told 'im it was. Look—you're with Staccio, right?"

The guy dumbly nodded his head.

"No offense, don't read it that way. But I didn't come all the way from LA to sit in the woods and swat mosquitoes. I told Augie that. You just don't send Black Aces out to crack their knuckles in the woods."

The guy was stumbling along the trail, half a pace ahead, semi-propelled by Bolan's firm grasp on his arm. His head jerked around at that "Black Aces" bit, the light of revelation dawning there. "That's right, Mr. uh Ruggi,' he muttered. "I don't blame you for feeling that way."

"Call me Frank."

"Sure, Frank. So you told 'em where to get off."

"I told Joe Staccio where to get off."

The torpedo was grinning appreciatively. "Augie made 'im call you, eh."

"Let's just say that we came to an understanding," Bolan told him with a chuckle, eyebrows arched in secondary meaning. "Joe's all right, don't read me wrong. This just isn't his cup of tea, that's all. He should stick to his rackets. That's where he's king."

"You're certainly right, Frank. He is king there."

"No question about it," the "Black Ace" readily agreed.

A panel truck was parked at the edge of the woods—a late-model sedan just ahead of it, another across the road and poised to leap off in either direction. Two guys in Levis were leaning on shovels. A guy in a business suit and yellow hard hat was stationed at the bridge, another was strolling across. The guys with the shovels looked hot and irritable. A "work force" such as this was onerous duty, tiring, hard on the nerves. Each approaching moment could be an explosive one, and these guys had to stay up and ready for it. Bolan understood these burdens, and he'd learned long ago to make them work in his best interests.

The guys at the shovels were giving them an interested surveillance as they broke from the trees and approached the set. Bolan went directly to the panel truck and sat in the open doorway.

He handed the ID wallet to his companion and said, "Tell Larry I want to parley."

The guy said, "Sure, Frank," took the wallet, and headed for the car at the other side of the road. He flashed the open wallet at the shovel-leaners as he ambled past them. The guys exchanged glances then sent curious gazes toward the visitor. Bolan sent them not a look, but both became immediately uncomfortable and started halfhearted digging motions with their tools.

"Larry" turned out to be one Lawrence Attica, a crew boss in Staccio's Syracuse arm. They had never "met"—but Bolan's mental mug file clicked to an immediate make.

The guy came hurrying over, carrying the ID wallet like it was an explosive device. He returned it with a flourish and a beaming smile. These guys did not often meet a Black Ace—a troubleshooter from *La Commissione*. Such honors were usually reserved for the higher ranks, though it was generally known that the men with the Black Ace IDs frequently operated incognito within all family groups.

"Mr. Ruggi, it's a pleasure," Attica said, almost turning inside out with his smile. "Georgie tells me you been across the river all this time."

Bolan showed the guy an ironic smile as he replied, "Larry, don't ever believe it when they tell you that some day you'll be leaving the shit details behind you."

The crew boss howled with much more appreciation than the humor deserved.

"How are things in Syracuse?"

Attica made a so-so gesture with his hand. "Town's getting out of control, Mr. Ruggi." He snickered. "Too much crime in the streets."

Bolan grinned at that and told him, "My name is Frank."

"Sure. Thanks. Uh, what's this Georgie is saying? We're pulling out?"

Bolan grinned on. "Don't you think it's about time?"

"God yes! These shit details send me up the walls, Frank."

"Call your boys in. Tell 'em it's time to go get laid."

Attica beamingly passed the chore on to Georgie who was apparently the number-two man in the crew. It took less than a minute to break camp, as there were no dragging feet in that regard.

"You got a way into town, Frank?" Attica wanted to know.

"Glad you mentioned it," the Black Ace replied. "I'm leaving my partner in the area. He might need the car."

"Hell, it's an honor—we got plenty of room. You ride with me." Attica snapped his fingers at the second in command. "Georgie—it's just me'n Frank in the Chevy. You take the boys back. See you at the hotel."

Georgie smiled at Bolan and went his way.

And Bolan went the way of all of them—as honor guest of the crew boss from Syracuse—directly to the Mafia Arms of Montreal.

And, sure, *bravura* was the word.

7: ACES UP

Since leaving Vietnam, Bolan had developed
the military concept of "role camouflage" to a
high art. To "be seen but not discerned" was the
basic premise of any camouflage job. Role camouflage went a step farther and involved quite a bit
more than mere physical disguise. The method
school of acting taught similar techniques—and
perhaps Bolan was, after all, a consummate actor
and a master of disguise. The "disguise" itself,
though, was always finely subtle and came mostly
from within the man.

Simply put, in Bolan's own words: "Perception
and recognition occur entirely within the mind.
It's a pretty frail faculty for most humans. Show
them something very familiar and they will leap
to an automatic identification. That's one of the

problems of our society. We leap to identify from the flimsiest perceptions. Long-haired people must be hippies. Short-haired people are rednecks. Cops are pigs, young people are always screwed up, anyone past thirty is senile. That's human perception. And that's what makes role camouflage work."

It worked beautifully for Mack Bolan. By the time they reached their destination, Larry Attica would have gladly killed for him—at the snap of a finger. He even told him so: "Listen, Frank you can depend on me. I know you got a tough job and it must get pretty lousy sometimes. But I want to say this, and I mean I got to say it. You're an all-right guy. You need something done, you just look at me and snap your fingers. You get what I mean."

Bolan had it, precisely. "I got a feeling you won't be around Syracuse much longer," he told his new disciple. "And I guess *you* get what *I mean.*"

The irrepressible smile beaming from Attica's self-satisfied face signified that he certainly had it. The guy was a third-echelon ranker in a more or less second-echelon organization—young enough to want more, old enough to have started entertaining worries that he never would. Association with a Black Ace was gift enough from heaven; to find favor and patronage from such an exalted one was heady stuff, indeed.

The hotel was not Montreal's largest but it cer-

tainly qualified as one of the finest. A uniformed
doorman took the car at the curb and ran it down
for further handling by parking attendants. It
was mid-afternoon but the lobby was filled with
arm-waving conversation and good nature. There
was not a woman in sight. Hard-looking guys
stood in clumps everywhere, renewing old friend-
ships and forging new ones.

It was, in every sense of the word, a convention. A convention of criminals, despite the color-
ful banner proclaiming a welcome to the "World
Trade Association."

"Is the whole joint ours?" Bolan asked his companion.

"Rest of the week, yeah. Just be careful with
the help. They belong to the hotel."

Some guy in a checkered vest and Prince Al-
bert coat ran up and pumped Bolan's hand, murmuring something warm in a foreign tongue. Bolan said, "Yeah, yeah. How're things in Zurich?"

The guy laughed and went on to another hand.

Attica chuckled.

Bolan told him, "I don't want a lot of people
knowing I'm here. Not just yet."

"Sure. I understand."

"I get it that Staccio is the official host here.
Right?"

"Right, Frank. He'll be coming in late tonight."

Bolan understood that protocol. Staccio, as
stand-in for Augie Marinello, would be the last to
arrive—that is, the last official delegation to this

first international congress of crime. He told Attica: "I'll use Bobby Gramelli's suite. He won't be showing."

Attica clucked his tongue and said, "Yeah, I heard about that. Too bad. Bobby was an all-right guy."

They were working their way across the lobby. "I'll be working his shed," Bolan confided.

"Oh. I didn't know that."

"You're the first to know. I'll want you to round up all his crew chiefs and get 'em up to the suite one hour from now."

"Okay," Attica replied happily. "You want me to sit in?"

"You know it." Bolan gently slapped the guy's bottom and told him, "Go get the key, eh."

Attica grinned and took one step toward the desk. That was as far as he got before a smallish figure in hand-tailored threads stepped across his path.

"Larry Attica, isn't it?" the guy asked pleasantly.

"Yeah, oh—hey—Mr. Turrin. Pleased to see you. Hey, I want you to meet a—" Attica's gaze swept back to Bolan, the eyes asking the obvious question. Bolan nodded. "I want you to meet Frank Ruggi, out of the corporate office."

"I thought I'd seen you," Turrin said, neither hot nor cold as he acknowledged the introduction.

"This is Leo Turrin, Frank. Western Mass."

Bolan said, "Yeah, I know. Good to see you, Leo. Go get that key, Larry."

The guy grinned and hurried on with his mission for the "all-right guy."

Turrin lit a cigar, casting cautious glances about the lobby as he did so. "I don't believe it," he quietly declared. "I see it, but I don't believe it."

"It's what you don't see that counts," Bolan reminded his old friend from Pittsfield.

Leo Turrin had already invested several precious years of life in a quiet undercover operation for the federal government when Mack Bolan came blitzing into his world, an avenging angel bent on destruction of everything Mafia. With blood ties to the reigning regime, it had been a natural setup for the serious little fed with a Mafia-disgust which was at least equal in depth to Bolan's. The blitzer from Vietnam had proven almost too much for the man with a foot in each world. Bolan belonged to neither. Both of Turrin's worlds wanted the head of that guy—but it was a head which Leo Turrin had come to respect and admire, later to genuinely love, and the two had come out of the Pittsfield conflagration welded into a friendship that only death could dissolve.

It had been a dangerous game for Leo Turrin—even before Bolan. Now it was, half the time, pure insanity. The bosses of both worlds regarded Turrin as the foremost "Bolan expert" and frequently called upon him to assist in the apprehension of the fugitive (as identified in one world) bastard (as better known in the other).

Quietly, though, the two continued their close friendship and mutual support of the goals of each. Bolan fed Turrin and vice-versa. The arrangement had worked out very well for both. Bolan was still alive, with a pretty steady finger on the pulse of the enemy. Turrin was moving up swiftly in both worlds—now an underboss in Massachusetts and a highly prized, upper-echelon undercover operative for the US Justice Department.

Turrin had long ago thought that he was beyond surprise at anything the indomitable Mack Bolan might pull off. But he was not.

"You've got to be out of your head," he growled through the sudden cloud of cigar smoke.

"Same to you, friend," Bolan growled back. "Rest of these troops wouldn't know me from Mahatma Gandhi. You're right up on the block with me, now."

"We need to parley."

Attica was hurrying back, officiously twirling the key to the late Bobby Gramelli's hardsuite.

"Drop in any time," Bolan said to his old friend and partner at the knife's edge—adding, for Attica's benefit, "I think you've got me mixed up with someone else. Bring a bottle and we'll jaw it around."

Turrin nodded, rather coldly, and Bolan spun

off toward the elevators. Attica hung behind for a moment to polish another apple. He flashed the room number at Turrin and hissed, "He's a Black Ace, Mr. Turrin."

"That explains it," said the underboss from Pittsfield.

Attica hurried away to catch his new "sponsor." Leo Turrin watched the two of them enter the elevator. Then he tapped his cigar, sighed forlornly, and muttered, "Aces you've never seen yet, Larry." Then he ambled on across the lobby, resuming the check on his Bolan detail. It was, he'd long ago decided, a nutty world.

Joe Staccio had called him in Pittsfield, hardly twelve hours earlier, all in a lather. Mack Bolan was sure as hell headed for Montreal. Leo was the only guy in the whole organization who Joe could appeal to—nobody else, not nobody, could be entrusted with such an assignment.

It had already been cleared with the headshed.

Leo was to get it up to Montreal and take over the security arrangements for the meet.

Nobody else could be counted on to spot and stop that Bolan bastard. Bobby Gramelli was lying in his own blood in Buffalo, thanks to that same bastard, and Bobby had been the security chief. Up 'til then, of course, the security had been a pretty routine thing. Not now. The mere shadow of Mack Bolan, hovering above that do-all conference in Montreal, had changed everything.

Sure, Leo would be glad to go to Montreal.

Bolan was some kind of bastard, that was sure. Many people around the country were already convinced that the guy was some kind of damn phantom who came and went as he pleased, sat down and ate with them, joked and jawed and entertained them while setting them up for the knockover. Only Leo had lived through any of that.

Leo Turrin had quickly become the man of the hour in Montreal. In a week, or a month, or a year—if he should live so long—it was almost certain that Leo Turrin would be wearing a boss's ring. The value of that, in Washington, would be inestimable. Leo would be sitting in on the councils, participating in international strategy sessions, working all the angles from the very highest level of underworld authority.

It all came together to make things pretty tough for a guy like Leo Turrin. He loved that big blitzing bastard like a brother—more than that, even, he knew that Mack Bolan was a truly unique human being—an entirely selfless, comitted, all-together individual. He was a shining symbol to Leo Turrin of what a real man ought to be.

On the other hand, there was that sense of duty to Washington—Turrin's own commitment to an ideal, the ideal of justice under law, loyalty to a responsibility, service.

Yeah, it was a nutty world.

Mack Bolan and Leo Turrin were sharing the same suite for the Montreal Meet.

Aces, yeah—God! Aces like nobody had ever seen—and very probably would never see again.

It did not seem possible that Mack Bolan would be leaving Montreal alive. But—God!—what a way he'd picked to go!

Turrin smiled sourly at his own introspections and continued his appointed rounds. In life, so in death. Linked. The little underboss from Pittsfield had known it for a long time. Leo Turrin and Mack Bolan, when the time came, would die together.

Aces, yeah. In a dead man's bluff.

8: IN THE HOLE

There were two basic problems in Montreal to be approached. Of prime consideration was the big parley itself—the international meeting of crimelords designed to form the basis for *Cosa di tutti Cosi*. Bolan needed to break it up, to send the delegations scurrying back to their own turf. This was the minimal goal. It would not, of course, be enough. Like flies shooed from a piece of decaying meat, they would flock back at the first opportunity—or alight upon another likely victim—and business would proceed as usual.

A point of order needed to be made at Montreal.

And that would involve the other problem, the real one, for this troubled province. Bolan's problems with the mob itself were a large enough order. Even if he were disposed toward a meddling in the internal affairs of other nations, it seemed greatly doubtful that he could have any real effect upon the political and economic realities of French Canada.

Bolan was a realist.

He had not come to Canada to save Canada from herself, even supposing that he could do so. He knew, in fact, that he could not. He had come to make war upon the greater enemy—and this he knew he could do. The problem was: how best to approach the war so that the greater interests of Canada would thereby be served as well.

It was not really a soldier's decision—but, then, that was the only one he had available.

Unless . . .

He'd had that parley with Leo Turrin, while Attica was out rounding up the leaders of the security crews. He and Turrin had come to a general agreement regarding the conflict of roles being played by each, and then he'd told his old partner: "I want you to contact Brognola, Leo. You can tell him I'm here, but not what I'm doing. I'm not going to play Washington's games here but I would like to hear their recommendations. I want a full briefing—the militant angle, the labor unrest, the economic situation, the full range of US-Canadian relations as they now stand, all of it. And I want an intelligence packet, complete, the full treatment, nothing left out."

"It's a large order," Turrin replied gloomily.

"It's a large time. You tell Hal that's the only alternative I have to running amok here."

"I'll try," Turrin promised, then left—more disturbed than when he came in.

Now Attica and Joe Staccio's six hotshots were sitting there staring at him like he was chocolate cake and they were kids at a picnic.

"You boys relax," he told them with a grand air. "Get some drinks, light up, take off your coats. Let your peckers swing easy, then we'll get down to business here."

It was exactly the right thing to say.

The guys let it all hang out, "relaxing" far more than Bolan had a right to hope for, basking in the genial camaradie with a genuine Black Ace from the homeshed.

They spent a pleasant thirty minutes together, discussing the problems of security for such a large and important gathering. By the time the hotshots trooped out, all smiles and happy handshakes, the man from blood knew all their secrets. "Just keep it going that way," he told them. "You boys know your job. Don't let me bother you none. Just stay out of Mr. Turrin's hair. He's on special orders here, like me, and we just got to work around each other. You boys know how that goes."

Yeah, those boys knew. They were laughing it up all the way to the elevator. Bolan gave them a final wave and closed the door on that portion of the program.

The problem he was setting up was going to require some damn fantastic numbers, played to a precision pitch—and yet he could not realistically start the countdown until he received that intel from Brognola. There was, however, the ever-present hazard in this game of "aces up"—such a masquerade could not be carried on indefinitely. Each passing moment increased the hazard with geometric progression. He could not dally for long.

He checked the time and ran a mental calculation of the various probabilities. How long before Joe Staccio called to check the situation in Montreal—or how long before someone decided to call Staccio and verify the authority of Frank Ruggi, the man from corporate office? How long before some hotshot from another time and place ran head-on into a face he could not possibly forget? How long before . . . ?

Bolan sighed and tossed the calculations into the bosom of the universe. One fact was beyond calculation. He had not closed his eyes in rest for more than thirty-six hours. A guy could not run forever on determination alone.

He went into the bedroom, removed shoes and jacket, and lay down across the bed with the Beretta thumbed-off and ready—and then he eased his wearied mind into that torpor which he called "combat sleep": eyes slitted, systems idling but alert, intellectual centers at rest. Only "the animal" remained in that room. Mack Bolan, for the moment, had gone elsewhere. To the bosom, perhaps, of the universe.

He snapped back at full alert, nothing moving but the eyes behind those slitted lids. What had awakened him? How long had he slept?

He would not chance a look at his watch, but the changed lighting in the room told him that some hours had gone by; it was getting dark.

The sensing of presence grew stronger. He was mentally preparing for a quick flip off that bed when the girl edged quietly into the doorway. She stood there for a moment, gazing silently at him, then took a hesitant step inside.

His eyelids raised with the Beretta. "You didn't knock," he said in a flat voice.

Hers was shaky as she insisted, "Yes, I did. Like this." Timid, tiny knuckles beat a barely audible tattoo on the open door.

He chuckled and told her, "Okay, maybe you did. Why?"

"Why what?"

"Why did you knock?"

"Because I wanted to come in."

"But you came in anyway," he pointed out.

"Please put away that gun," she said, that pert voice still shaky.

She was a real honey. About five-five or -six, long dark hair, very unusual eyes, lovely skin. French. With a body that knew it. It was clad in a simple silk chemise, short-sleeved, hemming out about midway between hip and knee and gloating over the delicious treasures concealed beneath.

"Come here," he commanded roughly.

She advanced to the side of the bed. He twirled her around and patted her down, then sighed and holstered the Beretta. "See what a rotten world it is?" he growled. "Nobody's trusted, not even a beautiful kid like you. What're you doing here, anyhow?"

"I was sent," she replied, demurely casting those lovely eyes downward.

"Who did the sending?"

"The man in charge. I can't think of his name. He said you needed some relaxation."

Bolan the Bold did not believe that, not a bit. He'd seen them all, every size and variety, and this one just did not fit the mold anywhere. He said, "Okay, take it off."

Those eyes came up quick—cornered, scared, resigned all at once. "Can I—can I use the bathroom?"

"Who'd you say sent you?"

"The man."

"Attica?"

"Yes. Mr. Attica."

"He let you in?"

She nodded. "May I use the bathroom?"

"There's no windows in there, kid. Even if there were, it's a long drop to the ground."

"I-I don't know what you mean."

He smiled and stepped aside. "Straight ahead,"

he directed her. She paused at the open bathroom door to gaze back at him, then quickly slipped inside. The door clicked shut. Bolan sighed and picked up the telephone.

No, Larry Attica had not sent any broads to Frankie's room, but he'd be glad to do so. What type did Frankie like?

Frankie already had the type he liked, and he told that to his bosom pal from Syracuse—then he hung up the phone, gazed at that bathroom door, and wondered what the hell was coming off.

A silk chemise, as it were.

She came out in glowing flesh tones, and nothing else, and it very nearly took away the iron man's breath.

That first step had been taken with obvious, desperate bravado. Then she saw the look in Bolan's eyes, and the essential woman of her took over—as though maybe she was turning on just a little to the whole idea—and she aproached him the way a naked woman rightly should. But then, an arm's length away, it all deserted her. She stood there swaying, eyes brimming, biting at her lower lip to stop the darned thing from quivering.

Bolan had to turn away from that.

He went to the bathroom, got her dress, returned, and draped it across those shiny shoulders. "Just how far did you plan to carry this?" he asked gruffly.

"I need the money," she quavered.

"Baloney. You didn't come here for money, and Attica didn't send you. Who did?"

"I don't know what—"

"Get the dress on!"

She staggered back to the bathroom, bawling openly now. Bolan paced the floor and watched the door. Presently the sobbing ran its course. He heard the water running. A moment later she reappeared in the doorway, fully dressed, more or less composed, patting at her face with a towel.

He disgustedly told her, "You're the lousiest hooker I ever saw."

She shrugged and made a pained face.

"You want to tell me about it?"

"No. I can't."

He growled, "Okay. Good-bye."

"I can leave? You're not going to beat me up? Burn my feet with cigarettes?"

"Why would I do that?"

The kid smiled wanly and stepped back into the bathroom momentarily to carefully arrange the towel on the rack.

"Can I leave now?" she asked timidly.

"I told you to."

"Well then—do I *have* to leave now?"

He said, "Ah hell!" and went into the drawing room. The girl stood in the open doorway and watched him pour coffee from the Silex. "Want some?" he growled.

"Coffee? No. Thank you."

He took a pull at the coffee, made a face, and

gruffly told her, "You'd better beat it, kid. I don't know why you're here—and I really don't care why. But you're out of your element. Go home."

Damn. She was doing her best to hang in there.

"I-I'm sorry I chickened out. Can we . . . start over?" Nervous hands were plucking at that chemise again. "I promise—no more tears."

He said, in mild rebuke, "Don't do that"

"I—my name is Betsy Gordon."

He shook his head. "Doesn't fit. You're French."

"Half."

"You don't talk right."

"I went to school in the states for a while. Now I'm at the University of Montreal. Performing Arts."

He said, "Congratulations, but you won't get your diploma here. You blew it. Now blow out of here. I have things to do."

Those lush lips were quivering, about to let it all go again. Bolan turned to the window and growled over his shoulder, "What the hell is going on here?"

"You're not so tough," she challenged him in a breaking voice.

"Not *that* tough, kid," he assured her.

"You're not who they say, are you."

"Who do they say?"

"Super crook. In charge of everything."

He turned on her with a scowl, prepared to

scare the hell out of her. "C'mere," he snarled. "I'll show you who's in charge."

That damn chemise hit the deck again. Very little else was left for the imagination—a scrap of silk about two fingers wide at the base of that pretty little belly. He steeled himself and crossed to her in two huge strides.

Those eyes were two wide pools of downright terror.

And, hell, he just couldn't do it. He grabbed that long hair just below the skull and twisted his hand into it, jerking the lovely head into a hard angle. "Be glad I'm not who they say, kid," he said savagely. "I'd eat you alive."

He roughly shoved her into the bedroom, then snatched up the dress and threw it after her. She hit the bed and crumpled onto it, sobbing.

He was fighting down a strong impulse to go in there and comfort her when an insistent rapping at the front door stole the moment.

The girl's eyes came up with alarm and the tears shut down as though by a concealed switch.

Bolan's eyes flashed meaningfully as he instructed her, "Under the covers. Mess your hair some more."

He closed the door and crossed to the other side of the room. "Yeah, yeah—just a minute," he called to the impatient visitor in the hallway.

It was then that he noticed the chain lock. It was intact; that door was locked from the inside. His gaze traveled back to the closed door to the bedroom and dark things began tugging at the pit of his mind.

It was shaping into one of those damn nights.

A naked juvenile in his bed—for whatever confounding purpose—and very likely a shark at his door. A door through which no one had entered during the past few hours.

"Wait a minute," he growled loudly at the door, then he hurried to an inspection of the windows. He had already checked those avenues once but he had to do it again. The result was the same, however. There was no alternate path into this suite. Entry to the bedroom was only via the drawing room. Of course, that held for exists, as well.

He returned to the door and cracked it open, leaving the chain intact. "Who's there?" he growled.

"This is Joe," came the irritated response. "Joe Staccio. Let me in."

Oh yeah.

Sure.

Already it had become one of those nights.

9:   A BULLET FOR LEO

Joe Staccio was a *capo*. Not even a Black Ace threw his weight against a big boss—not openly, anyway.

Still, there were those unusual circumstances when he could. The Black Aces constituted a sort of Gestapo organization—a secret police, accountable only to the will and wishes of *La Commissione* which, itself, in the purely physical sense, was no more than a council of bosses. That council, however, was larger than the sum of all the bosses and much more than the whim or fancy of any individual *capo*.

The Black Aces were the physical manifestation of that larger spirit of *La Commissione*. They could, yes, take independent action against a boss. Mike Talifero gunned down Ciro Lavangetta in

Miami in a ceremonial execution which brought no repercussions onto the head of Iron Mike. Bolan himself, even, had carried it off against old man Angeletti, in Philadelphia.

It could be done, if done very delicately.

Chebleu's word, *bravura,* flashed into that moment of crisis as Bolan addressed the crack in that hotel room door.

"Joe! Great! I've been trying to locate you. Listen, I'm on the horn with you-know-who right now—but you and I need a parley. I want you to—"

"Open the goddamn door!" Staccio raged. "I'm not standing out here in the goddamn hall and jawing through a crack in no door!"

"Do what I say, Joe. Please. Are your boys with you?"

"Of course my boys are with me! And that's something I wanta know—why are all the road crews pulled back into town? What the hell is coming off here? I send boys to cover the map and I come back to find them slopping it up in Montreal."

The guy was in quite a lather.

"I called them in, Joe. The guy is already here, he's in town. Now here's what I want you to do. Get it up to the penthouse and park yourself inside solid walls. Stay there and—"

"Who the hell're you?" the boss stormed. "Where's Leo? What the hell is coming off here?"

"I just took a shot through the window, Joe—

not five minutes ago. Now get it up to the penthouse and do like I said. Aw hell—who's out there ... ?" Bolan already knew who was out there. The dapper figure of Little Al DeCristi had just moved through his line of sight. "Al? You there?"

"I'm here."

"Do it. Get Joe upstairs and put a shield around him. Don't take any shit off of him, just take care of him."

"Sure, I get you," the bodyguard replied tensely. "Come on, Mr. Staccio. You heard the man. It ain't safe here."

Staccio was spluttering a stream of obscenities. But the sounds were moving along the hallway, now, and Bolan knew that he'd made his point.

And he'd made himself some breathing room.

He pushed the door shut and headed for the bedroom. A ring of the telephone halted him in mid-stride. He scooped up the instrument and gave it a cautious "hello."

"This is Leo."

"Good for you. Guess who was just at my door."

"He's not now?"

"I deflected him to the penthouse. What's going?"

"Well I just called to say that he was back and to watch. I have that package for you. I'm coming up."

"Make it quick if you mean to see me."

Bolan hung it up and went on to the bedroom, prepared for a no-nonsense scene with the soft visitor.

There was no visitor.

She was not in the bed nor under it. She was not in the bath. She was not behind or beneath a stick of furniture in the joint. She was not on a window ledge because there were none. Other places where she was not included closets, dresser drawers, toilet bowl, and everywhere the dumbfounded mind of Mack Bolan could explore.

He was working on wall panels when Leo Turrin's soft knock put an end to the search.

"Hell's about to pop," said the man from Pittsfield as he hurried into the room. "Get it together and get out of here."

"I've decided to stay," Bolan quietly informed him.

"That's nutty and you know it."

"A lot of things seem nutty until you look closer. Leo, a beautiful kid somehow got in and out of this suite without using doors or windows. I wasn't dreaming and I wasn't hallucinating." He held up his hand and picked off a long, lustrous, black hair. "This place has secrets. I mean to find them."

Turrin handed over the intelligence package as he said, "I don't get. What the hell are you talking about?"

"Forget it. I'm staying. Now get out of here and let me study this package."

The underboss from Pittsfield made a worried face. "I don't know why I bother worrying about you. All of it isn't in the package, either. Best thing you can do is set a bomb and get out. Not a bad idea, at that. The intelligentsia of the whole world of crime is under this roof. You could probably count on getting at least half of them."

Bolan growled, "Sure, along with a hundred or so hotel employees, maybe a dozen firemen, and an entire square block of Montreal. What've you been smoking, Leo?"

"I was kidding," Turrin said, sighing. "But I'd almost go for it to put this bunch inside a flaming tower."

"Don't tempt me, Leo. What's not in the package?"

"First let's cover what *is* there. Hal telefaxed it up from Washington. I picked it up in the cover office here. Most of it is pretty bland stuff. The real shit is too harsh for commitment to written reports. Hal gave it to me on the scramble line. It will take me about an hour to repeat it to you."

"I'll settle for highlights," Bolan decided. "I may not have an hour, Leo."

"You may not have a minute, friend. I'll give it to you as brief as I can. But don't blame me if it comes out sounding like pure horseshit. Just believe me when I tell you that the conclusions are pretty well substantiated by the wealth of intelligence data I'm leaving out."

"So go," Bolan said, lighting a cigarette and

71

pitching an area of his awareness to that hallway door and beyond.

"First off, our relations with Canada are worse than they've been since the Revolutionary War. Many hard feelings stemming from many problems—balance of trade, fluctuating economies, Canada's almost total dependence on US markets and the shutting down of some of those—you know the gaff."

Bolan said, "Yeah. Let's get to the next plateau."

"Energy," Turrin reported sourly. "They don't like our pipelines from Alaska idea. They're shutting off our own sources of Canadian oil. And a lot of people are now shouting 'power to the provinces.' Picture forming?"

"Yeah. Go on."

"These are real headaches for the Canadian government, Sarge—not just paper ones. Quebec, now, is a special problem. Less than 20 percent of the total Canadian population is exclusively French-speaking. That constitutes a minority, on about the scale of our black people. For many of those, the quality of life is not much better. Montreal is the largest city in Canada—and most of the French-speaking population live in Montreal. Anti-American and anti-British feeling has been running very high here for some time. For a developing nation—which Canada certainly is— that's probably a pretty good thing if it doesn't get out of hand. That's the official feeling in

Washington, anyway. But right now the official barometer is reading a trade crisis, a political crisis, an energy crisis—the whole damn thing is in a state of crisis."

"And ripe for manipulation from outside," Bolan commented.

"That's the feeling, sure. For the people over in Justice, it's much more than a feeling. It's practically a conviction. Because of the other tensions, though, there's not too much flow of intelligence between Ottawa and Washington—practically none out of Montreal. The Canadian feds are here, sure, but they're intimidated by the fact that a Frenchman is Prime Minister and they don't know exactly where they stand between Ottawa and the *Quebeçois*. So we're not getting a lot of cooperation from Montreal. We didn't even know about this summit meet here until it filtered through our own sources."

"When did you hear of it, Leo?"

"Last night."

"It's that close, eh?"

"It sure is. I never knew the boys to be so clammy. Nobody knew except those directly involved in the preparations."

"So it sounds pretty big."

"It sounds downright colossal."

"What are the general conclusions from Washington?"

Turrin scowled and chomped his cigar. "It sounds pretty far out."

"I can take it. I probably already know. Confirm it for me."

"Takeover."

"Uh huh. The whole thing?"

"The whole damned thing, meaning French Canada. Staccio has been working very quietly up here ever since he came back from England. You remember that," the little guy added, with a sudden grin.

Bolan grinned back. "Yeah. What'd he do? Conscript the militants?"

"That's the feeling. Ever hear of QF?"

Bolan shook his head.

"*Quebeçois Français*. That's what goes for the national army of liberation here, now, since the big bust a few years ago that put the FLQ out of business."

"What's that FLQ?"

"Front for the Liberation of Quebec," Turrin explained. "Terrorist group, kids mostly. Kidnapped a British diplomat and Quebec's labor minister. The labor minister got killed. FLQ claimed responsibility. Wrong thing to do. They'd gone too far. The British don't dick around with that kind of shit. They rounded up the FLQ and jailed them all. End of a movement. That is, until the QF surfaced a while back."

"What has Joe Staccio been doing with this QF?"

"Leading them astray, probably. Hal has been reassessing the situation since we learned of the meet. It looks now like Staccio has been feeding them money and arms."

"In exchange for what?"

"There's your crisis," Turrin replied sourly.

"You said kids."

"Mostly, yeah. Seem to be taking their cues from some old dogs from the Vichy-Nazi days of the French occupation."

"These kids are well armed?"

"A lot of sophisticated weapons have been moving this way, Sarge."

"Uh huh. Okay. Thanks, Leo. You better get it up to the penthouse and cover your tracks with Staccio."

"I can hold off on that awhile. If you insist on keeping your ass flying here, well . . ."

"Don't wait too long, Leo. It's going to get grim."

"It's already grim," Turrin replied, sighing. "By the way, Hal wanted you to have something."

"Leg irons?"

Turrin chuckled. "Naw. He thought you might need a contact in the *Quebeçois*. He says if things get desperate, get to a guy named Chebleu. Andre Chebleu. Oh—you know the name?"

"Remember the Ranger Girls, Leo?"

"How could I forget?"

"Andre is Georgette's brother."

"Well I'll be damned. I never put it together."

"We're already in touch. He's been working the militant angle with Joe Staccio."

"Oh. Well. Okay. Hell, I don't know why you always ask me for intel. You seem to know it before any of us."

"Cover yourself, Leo. It's starting."

The little guy grinned. "Hell, I thought it already did."

Bolan walked him to the door, shook his hand, and shoved him out.

Some things made life worthwhile.

Leo Turrin was one of those things.

And Leo Turrin was, thanks to Bolan, at this moment in very grave jeopardy. He would have to figure the little big guy into every move he made, from this point forward.

In such a game, one of the ever-present options was that Bolan may—God help him—end up putting a bullet in Leo Turrin's head. If Georgette had drawn fifty days in the chamber, it was difficult to imagine what they would do to a "traitor" like Leo. And, yes, Bolan would award a bullet to his best friend in preference to seeing the guy go that way.

There had always been a bullet in Mack Bolan's gun for Leo Turrin.

And, he hoped, Leo carried one for Bolan, as well.

It was that kind of world, Mack Bolan's.

As the only option, perhaps, another strange world was now uppermost in Bolan's concern. It was a world in which cute kids with timid habits could pop in and out of locked hotel rooms without leaving a trace of the route of entry—and without leaving, even, a coherent hint as to the reason for the visit.

Quebeçois Français? Maybe.

He stared at the strand of raven hair—a rather flimsy object upon which to base so much of life and death.

He had to figure it out, make it work. Otherwise, bullets for both Leo and the Sarge could be the only option left.

He dropped his head to gaze intently at the strand of hair. A strand of the universe. A living substance, intertwining his life. A rope to freedom. Or perhaps a net for victory.

Where the *hell* had she gone?

And when the answer came—as he'd known it must—it was, of course, the only answer possible.

Betsy Gordon had come from the universal maze of cause and effect which had so impacted Bolan's life ever since that fog-shrouded cemetery at Pittsfield, so many, many lifetimes ago.

Yeah, and she'd escaped back into it.

All that was left now, for Bolan, was to find the doorway—and to find it quickly. Otherwise, he'd have to start preparing that bullet for Leo.

Nothing else would do.

He *had* to find that doorway!

10: ROLL CALL

"What the hell do you think I am?" the boss fumed. "A stupid old man? Huh?"

"God no, Mr. Staccio," DeCristi purred. "Nobody never said nothing like that about you."

God no. Not about Joe Staccio. In the first place, he wasn't old. Fifty-eight wasn't old. Joe was still a bull, hard as nails, tough as they come. And no guy who'd managed to survive forty years and more in *this* business could be called *stupid*. God's sake. Never mind just surviving, but coming up the road Joe had traveled, to become *boss*—and a respected one, at that. What the hell, some day Joe Staccio would be the number-one boss in the whole country—probably even in the whole world.

"I think you're the greatest guy I ever knew,

Mr. Staccio," the loyal bodyguard assured his boss. "It ain't disrespect, sir. I just worry about you. It's my job to worry. You wouldn't want a tagman that didn't worry."

"You're right, Al," the boss told him, relaxing a bit. "It's been a tough day. I guess I got too much of my ass in this thing."

"You'll get back away from the windows, huh Mr. Staccio?"

The boss chuckled and said, "Sure, Al—you know what's best, eh." He stepped away from the glass wall of the penthouse apartment and dropped into a leather chair near the bar. "Get me some wine. Chianti. Bring the bottle. And bring me the phone. I'm gonna get to the bottom of this business and damn quick. Who the hell is this guy Ruggi? I never heard of no Ruggi, Al. Have I?"

"I don't think so, boss," the bodyguard replied. He'd moved behind the bar and was inspecting the wine rack. "Course—we never know about those guys. Frankly, I don't like it. I think it's a bum setup. Give those guys a license to change their faces and their names any time they feel like it, give 'em a license to come and go as they damn please, a license to—well, it's a bum setup and I don't like it none."

"You know how those things get started," Staccio said, sighing.

"I bet you know how to stop 'em too, boss."

"Welll ... things have gone to hell, Al, since

Mike Talifero bit the dust. I think it's time for a change."

DeCristi brought the Chianti and a sparkling glass. He gave the glass to the boss, draped a towel over his arm, popped the cork, and poured the wine. "Mike was a real iron ass, wasn't he, boss?"

"Not iron enough, I guess," Staccio replied with a sigh. He sipped the wine. "Hey, they got pretty good juice here, Al. Try it."

The bodyguard grinned and went to get himself a glass. He poured his own ration, tasted it, and said in a matter-of-fact tone, "This boy Bolan has taken a lot of ours, hasn't he?" The boss did not reply right away, so he added: "I mean, besides the Talifero brothers."

Staccio sighed and put his wine down. "He took my old friend Sergio. He took Deej—who I never really gave a shit for, anyway. Then he took— let's see, just at Miami he took Johnny the Musician, George the Butcher and Ciro—you gotta count them, 'cause he really set it up." The boss was counting them off on his stubby fingers. "He took Arnie the Farmer and most of his headmen. He came stompin' into New York and took Freddie Gambella—and boy wasn't we all surprised about that. He took Don Gio at Chicago, not to mention Pete the Hauler and Larry Turk and Joliet Jake—shit, he wiped Chi clean. He got Pat Talifero at Vegas." Pained eyes raised to the wine glass and the boss from upstate took another taste of wine. "Pat's a vegetable, they say. Same as dead, I wish he was. Mike never got over that. I think that's what killed his nerve, and it damned near got Augie killed in the bargain."

"Who else did we lose?" De Cristi prompted, his own face screwed into the effort.

"Aw hell, Al. Stop counting. It's terrible. Quick Tony Lavagni. Old man DeMarco and Tony the Tiger Rivoli. West Coast—I didn't know them very well. Tony the Tiger, they say, was a crazy man. Some of the guys, Bolan did us a favor. But then there was men like Books Figarone, Manny Greco—an old friend—Guarini, valuable man, big loss to the combine. There was Smilin' Jack Lupo, hell—on and on, Al. Yeah. We lost a lot to that boy."

"I was just thinking of the bosses," DeCristi said. "How 'bout Angeletti, in Philly. Mr. Vincenti, at Detroit. Marco Vannaducci. Eh? God, he had a right to die in bed, boss, old as he was."

"Yeah," Staccio said sadly. "Get me that phone, Al. I got to make some calls."

The roll call of the dead had produced a profound effect on Little Al DeCristi. He got the phone and placed it on the table near the boss's knee then went to check the palace guard—feeling down, very down.

He had ten good boys up here, as a living shield for Joe Staccio. And he wished he had ten more. He wished, more than that, that he could just

81

pick the boss up and carry him downstairs, put him in the car, and blow this damn place entirely.

Mack Bolan was a goddamn kingslayer.

Al DeCristi did not wish *his* king slain.

That guy Bolan was a walking disaster. Somebody needed to *stop* that guy. Walkin' around like he had a damn license—a license ... yeah, like a guy with a *license*.

DeCristi ran out to the terrace and tapped his number-two boy. "Get back down there," he growled. "Check that Ruggi guy. I don't like his smell. Haul his ass up here, and I mean *haul* it if you have to. Kick the damn door down, anything you have to do. But get him up here."

"I'd better get some backup boys, Al."

"Take all you want, but not from here. Get it moving."

The kid hurried off, and DeCristi continued his anxious rounds.

Two minutes later, he was convinced that everything looked swell—all the boys were on their toes, ready, even a bit anxious to see something going down.

But the chief bodyguard still did not feel right.

He returned to the lounge and quietly approached the boss. He was sitting just as DeCristi had left him though slumped over a bit, the wine glass on the table, telephone in his lap.

It had been a rough day, yeah. Maybe Mr. Staccio was getting a bit into his years, at that.

DeCristi had never known him to fall asleep at the switch, like that.

But then something harsh and unmovable lodged in Little Al's throat, something worse than that post-mortem roll call, something that sent him quivering and shaking all over. He moved jerkily to the chair and placed a hand on Joe Staccio's lolling head—and then he let out a screech which was heard throughout that penthouse.

Joe Staccio was dead. He was very, very dead. His throat had been cut from ear to ear.

And that wine glass, the one which Little Al had filled with Chianti such a few unbelievable moments ago, now contained a chillingly familiar object.

It was metal—an iron cross, with a bull's eye at its center.

The kingslayer had struck again.

Joe Staccio had answered roll call.

Things, in Montreal, had definitely "started."

11:   FLIGHT PLAN

Leo Turrin came charging into the penthouse behind a wedge of bodyguards, responding to the mournful screeches from within and wondering what the hell was going down in there.

Little Al DeCristi was standing over the still form of Joe Staccio, holding the head with both hands and bawling like a baby.

Turrin took charge immediately, sending the inside men to a quick search of the apartment and pulling Little Al off of his dead boss.

"Jesus what happened here, Al?" he asked, not exactly feigning the shocked tone.

"His throat, his throat—Christ, Mr. Turrin— why'd he have to do it that way? That ain't no way to . . ."

Leo had not exactly been "friends" with Joe Staccio. They'd had a business relationship, a few times—that was it. But he could not help being moved by the genuine anguish of Little Al De-Cristi—the upstater's number-one tagman for more than ten years. Any number-one boy of that long a standing would be much more than a mere bodyguard. He would be friend, confidante, man-servant, mother-hen. Sure, Leo Turrin could appreciate such anguish.

"Who did it, Al?" he asked mildly.

"The bastard did it." The tears were still flowing. "And I know who he is. I mean *really*. And I'm gonna cut his heart out, Mr. Turrin. I got rights, and he's mine."

"Sure, sure," the Pittsfield underboss agreed soothingly. "But who're you talking about?"

Tortured eyes swept to the medal in the wine glass. "Him."

Turrin said, "Aw hell."

"I know who he is. He's that Ruggi guy."

Larry Attica had just come running in. He squalled, "*Jee-*zus! Ruggi did this?"

"Al is all tore up and don't know what he's saying," Turrin explained. "Ruggi couldn't have done this. He's down in his room. I just came from there."

A crackle of gunfire sounded from the terrace, abruptly diverting all attention to that area. Little Al, tears and all, was the first to come un-

85

stuck. He had gun in hand and was two paces across that room before Turrin and the others found their reaction.

When Leo Turrin arrived at the edge of that lighted terrace, the whole story was there in frozen frame and living panorama. Standing atop a brick wall about ten feet from the building's edge was the tall man in black, standing large in the silhouette and methodically blowing hellfire and thunderation from a hand howitzer. Two guys lay sprawled in fluid along the patio and another had just lunged shrieking into a potted tree.

Little Al had his own cannon up and talking in rapid fire. The fire from that black silhouette tracked across swiftly to pick up on that threat and three fast rounds whistled past Leo Turrin's nose and buried themselves in the wall behind him.

He hit the dirt, fast, and threw a couple of rounds into the air, just for the show.

Little Al was reloading his revolver on the run and charging the wall. The big guy up there saw him coming, and let him until the last possible moment—then he parted Little Al's hair with a hot zinger.

The little guy took a tumble and went on rolling across the artificial lawn. Turrin briefly watched that plunge—and when he lifted his eyes again to the wall, the fantastic man in black was no longer there.

The firing had ended with eerie abruptness.

Larry Attica showed his head at a patio post and called over, "Mr. Turrin! You okay?"

"Yeah, I'm okay," Turrin growled back. "Where'd he go?"

"Christ, I dunno."

Turrin gave it a five count then sighed and issued the standard command. "Check it out!"

"Yessir. You boys move it on out there. Keep it down, keep it *down*. Charlie—take some boys to the other side. We got the bastard this time! Don't let 'im off this roof!"

Grimly quiet men were scurrying all about that lighted roof, now. Turrin got to his feet and stood there in silent contemplation of the battlefield.

What the hell could he do now?

The Sarge had torn it.

There was no damn way out of this.

He took a dispirited walk to the twitching figure of Little Al DeCristi. The guy was groggy and there was a shallow furrow along his scalp—but that seemed to be about the extent of it.

"Did we get 'im?" were DeCristi's first words.

"I think so," Turrin said quietly.

"I guess I went crazy, Mr. Turrin."

"Naw, you were great," said the up-and-comer from Pittsfield. "And you got it lucky. The guy only gave you a quick kiss."

"I was lookin' right up his barrel."

"Count your blessings, then," Leo the Pussy advised the lucky tagman, and he went on back to the apartment.

He was gazing dejectedly at the remains of Joe Staccio when Attica came in, scowling.

"I don't understand this," the crew boss reported, "but that son of a bitch ain't out there. He ain't nowhere. I even had the boys link hands and sweep it, parapet to parapet. How the hell does he do it?"

Another man came in to report to Attica. "No ropes, no grapples, no sign of anything, Larry."

"Check the ground below," Turrin muttered.

"It's fifteen stories down," Attica pointed out.

"That's the idea. Maybe he fell over."

Attica snapped his fingers, sending two of his crew to check that possibility.

Little Al wandered in, his eyes dazed, an ooze of blood sliding along his forehead. "You sayin' we didn't get him?" he inquired of no one in particular.

Attica told him, "It looks like he maybe pulled it off. We're still looking, Al. Geez, I'm sorry about the boss. This is terrible."

"I'm gonna settle something once and for all," the little guy said. He was checking his pistol. "You wanna go with me, Mr. Turrin?"

"Where we going?" Leo asked, brow furrowed, eyes worried.

"I think we should look at that room down

there. Your room. *Ruggi's* room. I'd like to see what's in it."

"Go to bed, Al," Turrin said quietly. "You're not thinking straight."

"No disrespect meant, Mr. Turrin, but I never thought straighter. And I got to go see for myself."

"We'll all go," Attica suggested.

"Okay," said the man from Pittsfield, the Bolan expert. "Let's go."

And Leo Turrin knew how a doomed man felt, walking his last mile.

Attica was saying, "Until we all know exactly where everything stands, I guess I better speak for Mr. Staccio. Give me your gun, Leo."

"You crazy?" Turrin snarled. "What the hell do you think you're saying? And to *who?*"

"The gun, sir. I'm sorry. You know I gotta do this."

The son of a bitch was grandstanding, Leo Turrin knew that. There was no way he could howl the guy down. He was right and Leo was wrong. Even Augie would say so, at this very moment, with all the cards still in the deck.

He handed over the Colt and led the procession from the penthouse.

Last mile?

For damn sure. If that suite down there was empty, as Leo Turrin now knew that it must be, then there was but one sane way to go. He was mentally drawing that floor plan down there—re-

89

hearsing the choreography—planning his own death.

Last mile, no. Last flight. It would be about ten paces from the door to the window. And, yeah, he just might make it.

12:   NIGHTLIST

A guy whom Leo recognized as one of Staccio's palace guard, and three others, were pushing through the doorway from the stairwell when they reached the fifth floor. The kid did a double take on Al DeCristi and his face paled noticeably.

"You just now gettin' here?" DeCristi growled at the kid.

"Had to get some boys, Al. It's only been a minute."

"A damn long one," DeCristi fumed. He sounded now, Turrin was thinking, exactly like Staccio. "Stay right here. We might need you yet."

The kid nodded wonderingly, eyes on Little Al's bloodied head, but asked no questions. He and his boys stayed put while the others went on to the Ruggi-Turrin suite.

Turrin took a quiet look around, showing a smile he did not feel, then stepped up to the door and gave it a sharp rap.

Something *moved* in there.

Turrin swiveled his head with a sizing look for those behind him, then rapped again.

The door cracked open, on its chain, and Leo Turrin's heart began beating again.

"What d'you want, Leo?" asked that damned beautiful voice.

"Is everything okay in there, Frank?"

"In here? Sure. Why not?"

"We just had a thing up on the roof. Joe Staccio is dead. Some other boys, too. Just checking you."

Turrin turned away, his gaze harsh on Larry Attica. "I could understand Al going crazy," he snarled. "But you I don't figure, guy."

The Attica smile was pure sick. Little Al just looked perplexed. Turrin was turning them around and moving them away when the door opened fully and "Frank Ruggi" stepped out—fully dressed, even to coat and tie.

"Where the hell you think you're going?" he said. "You waltz up here and drop news like that then just turn and waltz away?"

"We, uh, we're trying to pass the word around, Frank," Turrin lamely explained.

"Get in here! All of you! Get inside!"

The three exchanged glances, then trooped inside. Ruggi followed, pulled the door shut and leaned against it, then said, "Now what is this about Staccio?"

Turrin found himself wondering who the guy really was—and he had known Mack Bolan in many roles. He went through the necessary "explanation" of the events topside while Little Al strolled the room in a seemingly aimless pattern and Attica just stood there looking sick.

"Tell it like it is," the man from Syracuse said, when Turrin reached the end of the tale. He handed over Leo's pistol, along with a contrite apology, then said to the Black Ace: "Al had a wild hair that maybe you and this Bolan boy is one and the same. He made the charge, Frank— and you know as well as I do, a charge is a charge. I had to check it out."

"Ruggi" appeared to be genuinely baffled. "Okay, swell, you did right to check it—but what's this thing with Leo's blaster?"

"Well, after all . . ." The third-ranker from Syracuse was clearly embarrassed. "He vouched for you, Frank."

"So did you," Ruggi snorted. "So what's that make you? Why didn't *he* take *your* gun?"

"Naw, you don't have it yet, sir. See—Leo knows this Bolan boy from way back. If you're really Bolan and he embraces you as someone else—why, then . . ."

"Ruggi" chuckled over that. Leo began chuckling, then Attica. Only DeCristi seemed unmoved by the humor in the thing.

93

"Joe ain't even cold yet," the little guy groused.

"Al is right, this is wrong," Ruggi said, abruptly returning to an appropriately sober mood.

"I see the hole in your window," Little Al said.

"You didn't believe it, eh."

"No, sir—frankly, sir—I got to wondering about that. I guess I get too jumpy when things are tight."

"You just stay jumpy, Al," Ruggi said solemnly. "It's your job to be jumpy."

"Thanks, Mr. Ruggi. I'm sorry about the mistake. I need to go back upstairs, now. The boss . . . needs me."

"Just another minute, Al," the Black Ace said. His gaze traveled between Turrin and Attica. "We got a bag of snakes here, gentlemen. This could blow this whole parley all the way back across the Atlantic."

"I'll call Augie," Turrin said.

"Maybe you shouldn't. Not yet." That cold gaze swept to the little bodyguard. "Al?"

"Yessir."

"You put Joe on ice. You know what I mean. Larry, you call your man down at the gendarmerie. Tell 'im some of the boys got a little high, had some target practice on the roof. You know, in case someone's calling in a gunfire report."

"Sure, Frank."

"Leo—you get us a copy of the VIP register.

94

I'll want double guards at all the important doors. But we tell nobody *why*. Get me?"

"Right," Turrin said, smiling sourly.

"Al—you're in charge upstairs. Tell all those boys to keep this quiet. No broadcasting at all. Got it?"

"Sure. Thanks, Mr. Ruggi. There'll be no broadcasts, count on it. But—well, sir—we got a bunch of dead boys up there."

"Ice 'em. We'll see they get proper attention when this thing blows over. You got any wounded?"

"Maybe a few with nicks."

"What's that you got there?"

"A nick, sir. Mr. Turrin says it was a quick kiss. I'd rather pass."

Ruggi smiled soberly and told the little guy, "A nick is sometimes the hand of grace, Al. Remember that. Get some medics up there to take care of the wounds. Just make sure they're quiet medics."

Attica said, "We brought our own, Frank. Right here in the hotel. Don't worry, they're quiet."

"Okay. You boys go get it together. Leo, stay. We got some hard skulling ahead."

Attica and DeCristi strolled to the door. "Watch your swingers," Ruggi told them, in parting.

Attica went out laughing quietly.

DeCristi paused in the open doorway to inquire, "You want some boys left outside here, Mr. Ruggi?"

"No, we'll take care of that ourselves," the Black Ace assured him.

"Be careful."

DeCristi pulled the door closed behind him. Bolan secured the chain lock and turned a wearied countenance to his friend from Pittsfield.

Turrin dropped into a chair and passed a hand slowly across his face.

Bolan lit cigarettes and passed one over.

"Bingo," he said softly.

"In spades," Turrin sighed. "How the *hell* did you do it?"

Bolan went to the wall separating the drawing room from the bedroom and lightly tapped it. "It's got secrets, Leo. I found them. Old air shaft, runs from roof to basement. Must have been here before they put in air conditioning. Sealed off now, not used. Almost."

"Almost what?"

"Almost not used. *Some*one has been using it."

"What d'you mean?"

"I mean a steel ladder running the entire length of the shaft—*new* steel. I mean a trick panel in this room—and God only knows how many more. I mean horizontal crawl spaces branching off from the main shaft at each floor level. Access ports at top and bottom—all new stuff—only the shaft itself is original equipment and it's been sealed off for a hell of a long time. How old is this building?"

Turrin shrugged. "Montreal's an old town."

"Well it's got some young ideas," Bolan assured him. "Listen, Leo, I think we can pull it. If we can keep the lid on just through the night—well, maybe there'll be nobody left to parley by sunrise."

"Hell, Sarge, there's several hundred guns in this building. Every damn delegation brought its own firepower. I don't see how you can expect to handle it on a piecework basis."

"I just want the bosses, Leo."

"Well, sure, but even then . . ."

"And I'm leaving no more death medals. That little thing at the penthouse awhile ago was strictly for stage effect."

"Yeah, I figured that. You were working my backtrack."

Bolan shrugged. "Had to."

"Just the same, it was too close. A dozen pieces were unloading on you there for a moment. You've got a charmed life, friend."

"I'm a charming guy," Bolan said, smiling sourly.

"Hey. I know what it took. Thanks."

"It took about three minutes."

"You could've done it in one—if you hadn't felt the need to show yourself, out there on the roof. That was pretty stagey, Sarge."

"It worked."

"Yeah. Oh yeah." Turrin held up his hand to show the shakes to his pal. "Damn near worked me into a premature grave."

Bolan chuckled, but it was not a pleasant sound. "Get it calm, friend. We have a hell of a night ahead. I want that VIP berthing list. I want the building plans for this hotel, all you can get and as far back as you can get without tipping our hand. I want a complete rundown on the QF, with a profile on every known or suspected member, present whereabouts, the whole gig. I want a standby hotline to Ottawa and one to Washington. I want a helicopter at my instant disposal—something on the order of a Huey. I want my cruiser brought over here from Bois des Filion. I want a police cordon at the airports, bus and rail terminals—nobody comes or leaves until morning. I want the telephone service to this building disconnected—with a proper cover story to go with it. I may want, later, a police line right out here on the street—with this whole building and everything in it sealed off from the outside world."

"Is *that* all you want?" Turrin asked, sighing resignedly.

"No. I want a sixteen-ounce steak and a pound of potatoes, tossed green salad with French, and a gallon of coffee."

"I don't know about the chow," Turrin said with a dour smile. "They're disallowing entertainment expenses now."

"And a company car, something really hot. A change of clothes, some shaving gear, and a toothbrush. Recent map of the city."

"Should I start writing it down?"

"That's all I want, Leo."

The little giant from Pittsfield tiredly got to his feet and headed for the door. He paused midway to look back upon the damnedest man he'd ever known.

"I know what you *really* want, guy," he declared quietly.

"It's what we both want, isn't it?"

"Sure, sure. And we'll find it. Someday. I thought I'd got there a little while ago. You took it back, Sarge. And look at what you give me in return. A list of wants."

"I want their blood, Leo," the big guy said coldly.

Turrin stepped outside and pulled the door shut. Sure. Leo the Pussy knew what Bolan the Bold really wanted. He wanted peace.

Peace.

What a hell of a word.

All it really meant, in the final analysis, was *death*.

And, sure, they'd both find that . . . sooner or later. They'd find it, probably, before sunrise.

13:   UNVEILED

The old section of the city known as Vieux-Montreal, with her ancient buildings and narrow, shop-lined streets, recalled Bolan's mind to New Orleans. Different situation, of course—different people—different time. He sensed a hostility here, an almost desperate atmosphere of human irritation.

The spirit, perhaps, of revolution.

Andre Chebleu lived in the neighborhood. He was as French as anyone here—and probably just as irritated with the way things were. But Chebleu was a Canadian fed. He was working the problems from the other approach—or so he would have Bolan believe. Nothing was ever that certain, of course. The odds were just as good for the other way. The guy could be a double agent—with the heavy flow of sympathy tipped toward the separatists.

Bolan had no interest in the politics of the thing. He had no feel for the situation and therefore no sympathies either way. It was a question for the Canadians to settle between themselves, this was his feeling. However . . . If the *Quebeçois* were in some sort of conscious alliance with the Mafia plans for Quebec . . . Then, yes, Bolan had an interest—and, of course, it mattered quite a bit if Chebleu was likely to blow in two directions at once.

Whatever the situation, it was time for the rendezvous and Bolan was cautiously feeling his way toward it. He made a slow pass of the neighborhood, then left the "company" car two streets over and returned on foot, strolling casually, sampling the vibes and scouting the physics of the place.

Street-corner conversations and radio-TV overflows from open windows were all in the French language, as were advertising signs and posters. People strolled about aimlessly—kids played in the streets—here and there a uniformed *gendarme* with a blank face and see-nothing eyes.

New Orleans, no.

Left Bank, Paris, was much closer.

The house he sought was set behind a wooden wall and a small courtyard. The gate was locked. Bolan pulled the cord of a small overhead bell and a young man appeared almost immediately from the shadows inside the wall.

"Qui est-ce?

"Je m'appelle Striker," Bolan replied, deciding to go with his rusty French. *"Je cherche Monsieur* Chebleu."

"Oui. Entrez."

The gate opened and Bolan went in. The kid looked about eighteen. He carefully secured the gate then inclined his head toward the house and led the way.

It was an old house, two-storied, very dimly lit. Odors from many generations of living cloaked its halls.

Bolan was shown to an austere, paneled room near the rear. A long table would seat perhaps twelve. Cheese, bread, and wine were set on a sideboard along the wall. The kid pulled out a chair and directed Bolan to the table. Not a word had been spoken since his entry, at the gate. Bolan accepted the chair, easing stiffly onto it. The kid went to the sideboard, sliced bread and cheese and poured a single water glass of wine, then placed the hospitality offering on the table.

"Moment," he murmured, and went out.

Bolan delicately tasted the cheese and tried the wine. Harsh stuff. He decided on a cigarette, and had barely got one going when Chebleu came in.

"Ah, wonderful," he said in quiet greeting.

They shook hands. Bolan asked him, point blank, "What is this place?"

Chebleu smiled and took a chair across from Bolan. The lighting was bad. Only about half of the guy's face was visible. "What does it seem?"

"It seems a monastery," Bolan said lightly. He grinned. "Or maybe you just don't believe in animal comforts."

"The purpose here is not comfort, you are correct," Chebleu replied. "It is a sort of headquarters."

"For what?"

"Freedom. Justice. Equality. Stale concepts, you may say. But very fresh ones here, *ami*. Very fresh ones."

Bolan said, "Yeah. How come they're precious only to those who don't have them, Andy?"

Something gleamed in those eyes. "Is food precious to the full belly?"

"What were you doing in Buffalo?"

"I told you."

"How about telling me again. From this empty belly, here, Andre. Tell me again."

The guy shrugged and turned his face into the shadow. "You know who I am and what I am. It was important that we know—" He slapped his chest for emphasis "—*we, we,* that *we* know the full price for all this cooperation from below the border."

"*Which* we, Andre?"

The guy lifted a hand and swept it at the empty room.

"I see," Bolan murmured.

"But, of course, there are *two* parents to every family."

"What kind of family are we talking about?"

"Call it the human family. First, *both* Adam and Eve. Mother and father. Quebec, also, is a child. A bastard child, perhaps—but even the bastard has both mother and father. France is but the father—an errant father, at that, a runaway parent. Mother Canada has certain rights, wouldn't you say?"

Bolan put out his cigarette.

Time creaked.

Presently, Bolan broke the silence. "Broken homes, they say, are very hard on children."

"I think so, yes," the Frenchman agreed.

"Must be damn tough trying to sort out the loyalties."

"I would say that, yes. But, then, there is always the middle ground."

"The toughest place," Bolan said.

"Thank you, yes. I believe it is."

"What are the feds going to do about this meet?"

"They are going to do nothing. Hands off. They watch. That is all."

"You've been in touch?"

"Of course."

"How about the Quebec police?"

"Also hands off."

"Why?"

The guy raised his hands and let them fall. "Indecision, mainly. There is the question of law. No great crimes have been committed, not obvious ones. There is also the question of politics. It is, as you say below, a hot potato."

Bolan grunted, "It is, as we say below, *clout*. Who's wielding it?"

"Guess," Chebleu replied softly.

"How deep does it go, Andre?"

"Deep enough to make cynics of an entire generation of *Quebeçois*."

"You mean . . . revolutionaries."

"Perhaps."

Bolan sighed. "Well, it's a young idea." He sighed again. "Also a very ancient one."

"In the cycle of power," Chebleu said, "sometimes a necessary one."

Bolan said, "Well, maybe this generation will find that middle ground." He rose to leave. "I kept the date simply because we had one. Also, to tell you that I will not be blitzing Montreal."

"No?"

"No."

"What, then?"

"A quiet night at the Mafia Arms. Then off to the next horizon."

"So."

"Yeah. By the way. I met a kid today. Saved my life. I'd like to thank her. Maybe you can help. She said her name is Betsy Gordon—but the name doesn't fit the frame. Definitely French, eighteen maybe twenty, innocent eyes, the guts of Jeanne d'Arc."

Chebleu stared hard at the man from blood, for a long moment, then replied, "Yes, I know her. I will give her your compliments."

"I need to talk to her, Andre."

The guy gave him another of those long stares, then he slowly got to his feet and stuck out his hand. "God favor you, Mack Bolan," he said quietly. "Thank you for friendship. Remain here a moment. I will send the girl."

There was no mistaking the sincerity in those eyes, but a conditioned wariness prompted Bolan to move into the shadows as Chebleu departed the room.

He checked his weapon and left it on the ready as he returned it to the sideleather.

It was a short wait. She must have already been in the house. A headquarters, yeah. She wore the same silk chemise, and she entered the room with that same quick grace he'd noted at the hotel.

The girl did not immediately see him. She looked around in some confusion, then started as he moved partially from the shadows.

"Hi," he said softly.

Still she could not get a good look at him. "You wished to see me, M'sieur?"

He moved fully into the light. "Don't vaporize on me, now."

She gave him the shocked reaction, staring

dumbly for a timeless moment—and, when she spoke, it was an incredulous whisper. "You? Mack Bolan?"

"Sorry," he said. "I didn't mean to play games with you."

A thousand thoughts were obviously chugging through that pretty head, questions answered, new ones forming—and, finally, horrified embarrassment.

He held a chair for her and suggested, "Sit down."

She did so, placing a tiny elbow on the table and lowering her head, face down, into the upturned palm. "I thought you were someone else," she mumbled into the hands. "At the hotel, I mean. Ohhh, I feel like a *fool*."

"Damned pretty one," he quietly observed. "Don't feel bad about the mistaken identity. It's a compliment to me. You said you were studying acting. True?"

"True," she said miserably.

"How'd I do?"

"Oh. Wow. Right up to the nitty gritty, you were great, just great."

"Like you," Bolan said kindly.

She giggled and raised her head to look at him. "I thought I would *die*!" she said, in a conspiratorial whisper. "When you said, 'Take it off!' Oh my God!" She shrieked with the memory of it, and Bolan was not sure that she was laughing or crying. A mixture of both, probably.

Anyway, the embarrassment was gone—and they were buddies who'd shared a delicious experience. They small-talked for perhaps a minute, then Bolan told her, "I need your help. Will you come back to the hotel with me?"

She raised luminous eyes to his and told him, "You know, I was scared to death you weren't going to ask."

14:   THE PROMISE

The name actually was Betsy Gordon. Her father was an American engineer who'd come north with the industrial movement, married a *Quebeçoise,* and made a permanent home in Montreal.

Though her father had done his best to anglicize her, the genetic endowment from her mother had proven the strongest. Betsy Gordon was very definitely a *Quebeçoise.*

She was a bit older, also, than Bolan had allowed her. With three years of college under her belt, she was certainly no "juvenile"—though there were those moments when he still had difficulty believing it.

She would not discuss *Quebeçois Français,* during that ride back to the hotel, in anything but the most general of terms—and she very deftly parried Bolan's expert probes into the political stance of Andre Chebleu.

Bolan did not mention her disappearing trick at the hotel, earlier, but he did inquire into the purpose of the visit.

She explained that readily. "That was supposed to be Mr. Gramelli's room. When Andre returned with the news that Gramelli was dead, we thought it would be a good idea to have a look at that room."

"We?" Bolan prodded.

The question merely provoked one of those girlish responses. She giggled and said, "That room was supposed to be empty. I nearly died when I saw you lying there with a gun on me. I thought, at first, that Gramelli's death had been greatly exaggerated." She laughed at her little joke and added, "I thought I was a goner, for sure. I decided, very quickly, that it was time for Betsy to grow up and become a woman."

He gave her a studied gaze, then commented, "You've been resisting that, eh?"

"I suppose," she said, tossing her head in the reply. "I guess it's easier to be a kid. But I thought for sure, for a while there, that I was going to *die* a kid." She giggled again. "Now that's not exactly the same as *being* a kid."

"So you decided to pose as a hooker."

Those eyes danced. "First thing that came to

mind. What is that—a Freudian commentary on the true role of women?"

Bolan chuckled at that. "Sounds more to me like the will to survive."

"Same thing, isn't it?"

He looked her over from a fresh viewpoint, then told her, "I think maybe you're a better actress than I realized. Were those tears genuine?"

The giggly mood had vanished.

She waited a moment to reply, then told him, "Well, let's say that they were inspired."

Son of a gun. He was remembering how quickly the waterworks had shut down when Joe Staccio knocked.

"Suckered me, didn't you?" he said quietly.

"I thought you were a mobster," she explained. "Maybe even Gramelli's replacement. I figured, heck, I was there, wasn't I? I may as well find out what I could."

He said, "Without sacrificing too much in the bargain."

"Well ... I sensed a—a sort of gallantry or something in the way you were—I mean, I thought I could handle it."

"You did," he told her. "Very well."

"Well ... to be honest, I *was* scared silly." She giggled, bringing the kid back. "I'm really not that good an actress—not yet."

Bolan was not so sure of that.

He withdrew into silence and was rethinking

the entire Betsy Gordon question when she asked him, "What sort of help do you need from me?"

He thought about his answer for a moment, then told her, "I want you to show me how to get into that hotel without being seen."

She twisted in the seat to give him a fixed gaze. "You found the passageway."

He nodded. "Part of it. I need the full layout."

"Why?"

He decided that he would have to take Betsy Gordon on faith. "You know what's going on at that hotel?"

"It's a meeting of mobsters, isn't it?"

"Do you know *why* they're meeting?"

She replied, "That's what we've been hoping to find out."

"Andre hasn't told you?"

"Told us what?"

"About the nature of the Montreal Meet."

"Does he know?"

Bolan sighed. She was playing it mighty cozy. But, after all, why not? Who the hell was Mack Bolan to her?

There was no time for cute games. He told her, straight out. "The mob is trying to engineer a takeover in Quebec. Not an underground takeover but a total one. My intel says that they're in some sort of alliance with a local militant group, that they intend to subvert this group to their own purposes. Montreal is to become the crime capital of the world. This meeting that's scheduled to

112

take place tomorrow will formalize that plan. I mean to stop it. I've established an identity at that hotel. But I need to do my work without being seen, otherwise the whole thing will crumble away. They'll simply regroup somewhere else and go on with the cannibalization of this province. I figure I have one chance, and I guess it all depends on you. Can you show me the secrets of that place?"

She said, "I—I need authority to do something like that."

"Where do you get it and how long will it take?"

The girl sighed and twisted about in agitation on the seat.

"I trust you, Betsy. Can't you understand that I have a singular interest in this town? I am not your enemy. I could be your only hope. These people who are here now will not be benevolent or even humane masters. You've got to trust me, and you've got to help me."

"I—dammit, I ... it would require a vote. From all who—a vote. Tomorrow, maybe."

"No way," he said. "I need it tonight, right now."

She was gnawing her lip, head averted, staring fixedly out the window.

"Trust your instincts, Betsy," he said quietly.

He stopped the car, following another moment of silence, and told her, "Sorry I don't have time to take you back." He was digging for his wallet. "I'll give you cab fare."

"Put it away!" she said savagely. "Let's go, let's go!"

He smiled soberly, put the car in motion, and said, "Yeah, it's much easier to be a kid."

"Just go! I suppose you want the secret way in."

"I sure do."

"Okay. Go two blocks east, toward the river. We start in the sewers."

"That's a likely place," the Executioner muttered.

"That," said the young revolutionary, "is my sentiment exactly." Those eyes flashed, and Bolan knew that this was no act. "One word of warning for you, Mr. Bolan. You may have great success in your war against mobsters. Betray us, however, and you will find the meaning of war."

Bolan had no comment to that.

He believed her.

to take you back . . . . his wal

. . . . "Tech

. . . .

15:   THE TREE

The old hotel had been built quite a few years
before the modern concepts of central heating
and cooling became an architectural reality. New
owners began a remodeling program in about the
year of Betsy's birth. Her father's firm were the
engineering consultants during the modernization
of the old building, and again very recently during a major refurbishing in preparation for the
1976 Olympics.

Bolan could elicit no details into the "how" or
"why" of the fantastic system of secret passage-
ways which now honeycombed the building.

"No. My father knows nothing of this."

"No. The mobsters know nothing of this."

"It is ours. We did it. Ask no more."

The "we" remained also a mystery—although

Bolan, of course, had his own thoughts on the matter. Betsy Gordon was quite obviously a member—perhaps even a leader—of the separatist organization known as QF.

They went over the building plans which Leo Turrin had deposited in Bolan's room and the girl superimposed onto the blueprints, from memory, a detail of the hidden routes.

Bolan had been fairly accurate in his early assessment of the system. It did, indeed, cover the entire building—though obviously much of the work was not complete. Even so, direct secret access was available to about 25 percent of all the guest rooms and to every level of the building.

He gave the girl a respectful gaze and asked her, "How the hell did you do it?"

"The Chinese have a saying," she replied enigmatically.

"Which one?"

"Did you know that there are five million Frenchmen in Quebec?"

"That's quite a few."

"Yes. Suppose each one picked up a brick. How large a building do you suppose we could erect?"

He asked her, "How many did it take to refurbish this hotel?"

"We are legion," she said, and strolled to the window—ending that line of conversation.

Bolan ended it also. He was satisfied, for the moment, that the girl was cooperating right up to the wall of her other loyalties—and it did not seem likely, at this point, that there would be an occasion for conflicting loyalties.

"I'm trusting you with my life," he quietly reminded her.

"Big deal," she said, without turning around. "Coming from a man who flings his life about in gushes and squirts, it doesn't seem a very important trust."

"It's important to me."

"Sometimes I wonder," she mused.

Bolan understood that. It was an international sentiment, shared on occasions by all those who live on the heartbeat. Mack Bolan and this girl had quite a lot in common. He told her, "Self-doubt is one of the occupational hazards. It's healthy, if you don't lose yourself in it."

Her voice was small and almost whispery, that pert face all but shrouded in the shadows of the night. "It gets very hard, sometimes, to separate right from wrong."

"All the time," he corrected her.

"What's right about you, Mack Bolan?"

He said, "I never ask."

"Afraid of the answers?"

He shook his head. "Afraid of the question. The answers all come out the same, in the end."

She turned to face him, then, arms folded at her breast, eyes gleaming at him from the gloom at the window. "I guess I lost you there, somewhere."

"You never found me, kid."

117

"I tried. I've been trying all evening."

He sighed. "And every time you look at me, you see yourself."

"Maybe," she admitted.

"You don't like what you see."

"I guess that's what I'm trying to sort out," she said softly.

"A mirror image can be confusing," he said. "The left hand looks like what the right hand is doing. It gets even worse when you look for yourself in another. It bothers you that I wade in human blood."

"Yes."

"And you wonder: 'Is that what I am going to become?' It's the question that shakes you. The *question*, not the answer. You haven't even arrived at the answer, have you?"

Her lips formed the "No" but there was no articulation.

He waited a moment, than asked, "How good are your weapons?"

"Very good," she whispered.

"How strong are your people?"

"Very strong."

"Abe Lincoln gave the answer to your question, Betsy, a hundred years before you were born. He told us that revolutions do not move backwards. Will you become like me? Yes, if you live so long. Will you ever know right from wrong? No, not unless you die too soon."

"That's pretty heavy," she told him.

"So is war," he said quietly.

"I need to ask you. I've never had the opportunity to ask a master. Does it bother you?"

"Killing?"

"You sit here, going over these plans, like a cold machine. It isn't a war you're mapping—a glorious war, with drums beating and bugles sounding—it isn't a dash across the plains with banners unfurled. It's pure and simple murder. You plot deaths by the hundreds. Doesn't it *bother* you?"

Bolan lit a cigarette and turned away from that searching gaze. Of course it bothered him. What did *bother* have to do with it? He quietly told her, "It sounded like you were describing the Charge of the Light Brigade. That was an actual event, you know. Happened in the 1850's. The French marshal, Bosquet, was there. Know what he said?"

"Something fitting, I'm sure," the girl murmured.

"Depends on your point of view. Bosquet said, 'It is magnificent, but it isn't war.' So you tell me, lady guerrilla. What *is* war?"

"Let's get back to revolutions," she said tensely. "And stop lecturing. I don't need a —"

"You don't like answers, do you? Just questions. You can play with questions for the rest of your life and never have to worry with answers. Look at me, Betsy. Here it is. I am your answer. Look at it."

"I—I better be going."

"I think you're right. Thanks for your secrets, Betsy. Forget the lecture, huh? You'll find your answers—your way."

She had gone to the escape panel. She turned back to look at him as he spoke the parting words—and, for that final moment, there, the kid was back. "I—I guess I'll stick to the questions," she whispered—and then she was gone.

"Yeah," Bolan sadly said to the blank wall. That was precisely what worried him about young revolutionaries. They played with politics, not war. Questions were great stuff, for the classroom.

On the field of combat, though, questions became answers. Suddenly. Finally.

A war was never a question.

War, this master knew, was an answer—good or bad, an answer.

And it could be a hell of a place to find a surprising one.

Leo Turrin arrived as Bolan was making his final review of the building plans.

"I see you found my package," the little guy said, for openers.

"Yeah, thanks, Leo. Come take a look at the eighth wonder of the world."

The underboss from Pittsfield strolled to the table, bit into his cigar, and took more than a look.

Bolan was explaining the markups: "Vertical shaft, see, roof to basement. Porthole at the bottom of the well—*voilà*—welcome to underground Montreal. These sewers interconnect. You could hide an army down there—and supply them from guess where." He tapped the blueprint. "It's like a tree—roots running underground, the broad trunk running up through the hotel center, branches everywhere."

"What the hell is it *for*?" Turrin growled.

"*Vive la révolution*," Bolan declared grimly.

"Then there really is something cooking."

"Looks that way. Did Chebleu file an official report with Ottawa?"

"Apparently he did. They've clammed up over there. Not a peep, not a rustle. We get it, though, there is some sorty of hush-hush cabinet meeting in session, has been since early this evening. The time coordinates."

"Yeah," Bolan said glumly. "Well—there's going to be hell to pay. I get the feeling that someone is being taken with the slickest con of the century. I just hope it isn't me."

"You contacted Chebleu, didn't you."

Bolan nodded. "Small comfort. I can't read that guy, Leo. I'm playing him strictly on instincts. I'd sure like to know what he told Ottawa."

"What did he tell *you*?"

"Damn little. He's been walking both sides of the street for so long, I get the feeling he doesn't know anymore which side he belongs on."

"Watch it," Turrin growled playfully. "You're touching mighty close to home."

"So you can appreciate the situation," Bolan said. "Suppose you and I had just met, just this minute. I know you're a fed. I also know you're a Mafia overlord. Now how do I know for sure *who* has infiltrated *whom*?"

"Yeah, I see the problem."

"As a further complication—I don't even know who the guy was representing with the Buffalo assignment. I mean, who sent him down there?" Bolan hit the blueprint with a fist. "This plan came from the same house where Chebleu is holing up right now. Okay—is there more than one French underground here? If so, which one is Chebleu playing footsy with? If not, who's sucking whom? The mob think they have a patsy militant group to do their dirty work here. The people who gave me this setup seem to hate the mob with all their guts."

Turrin mauled his cigar some more, then sighed and told his old friend: "It doesn't really matter. Does it?"

"I like to know who is the enemy, Leo," Bolan growled.

"Well, sure but—well hell, you can't take 'em all, Sarge. Come to think of it, I don't see how you can risk *any* move until you know where it's liable to take you."

"That's not my game, Leo. You know that."

"Yeah, but . . ."

"Every move takes me to the same place. I know where it's taking me—that's an answer that remains constant. The answer I need is the one that's up front, right here, right now."

"Yeah," Turrin agreed, sighing.

"Yeah is right. Who the hell is the enemy, Leo? Who am I taking there with me?"

The little guy sighed again. "I guess you find that out when you get there, Sarge."

Yeah. Sure. That much was obvious.

And Mack Bolan had long ago learned to be wary of battlefield surprises. Every instinct of his combat nature was screaming at him to break off, pull back, withdraw—leave the field for another time and place.

But there would probably never again be another opportunity such as the one presented to him here and now. The crimelords of the world were assembled beneath this one roof. They had come to divide the world among themselves, and then to devour it. The Executioner could not back away from this one.

He muttered something unintelligible beneath his breath and ran a hand across that blueprint.

"Was that meant for me?" Turrin asked. "If it was, I missed it."

Bolan smiled soberly. I said *C'est magnifique, mais ce n'est pas la guerre.*"

"I still missed it," Leo the Pussy said, grinning.

"It is magnificent, but it isn't war."

"Hell, I'm still missing it."

"Maybe someone else is, too," Bolan said quietly.

Yeah. But not Bolan. He'd found his answer.

16:   PUSHING IT

The time was midnight. All telephone service at the hotel had been "temporarily lost." Leo Turrin was in the penthouse, collaborating with Larry Attica on the problems of "guest security." Bolan's warwagon was in a private garage two blocks from the hotel. A Canadian Air Force helicopter stood at Bolan's disposal at a pad just minutes away.

The requested "hotline" to Washington had not materialized but a telephone in Bolan's suite—the only working phone in the hotel—was directly connected to an office in the Canadian capital of Ottawa where a joint US—Canadian "task force" headquartered.

Bolan had, also, his file of known or suspected members of *Quebeçois Français*—and a brief run-through was all that had been required to confirm his reading of the situation in Montreal.

Everything was ready for the push.

And so was the pusher.

He'd been to the warwagon and selected the weapons for the night.

The Executioner was combat rigged and ready. He wore the skintight blacksuit and quietshoes. The silent Beretta was in its customary place— shoulder-slung beneath the left arm. The big silver AutoMag, Big Thunder, rode the waist on military web. Slit pockets in the legs of the blacksuit held stiletto, garrotes, smoke sticks, flares. He wore special goggles and carried a small infrared flashlight in a special waist-holster which left the hands free for other matters.

The night was ready to claim her own.

Bolan entered "the tree" via the trick panel in his wall and descended quickly to the third-floor level, then crawled along a horizontal branch to the suite of Carmine Pellittrea, head of the Neapolitan delegation to the Montreal Meet.

According to the room chart, Pellittrea slept with a pair of bodyguards. Connecting suits to either side housed the rest of the group from Napoli, for a total of ten men. Not exactly the largest contingent at the congress but certainly among the most influential.

Bolan had not the faintest idea of what Pellittrea looked like but this did not really matter. It had to be a clean sweep, wall to wall.

He lay in the passageway with his ear to the panel for a full five minutes—getting the feel of life and movement inside there. When he did enter, it was with a rather valid understanding of what would be encountered inside that suite.

Entry was via the sitting room. The television was on, murmuring softly, providing the only light to the room.

A guy lay sleeping, fully clothed, on the couch. Another sat slouched in a straight chair, shoes off, feet propped onto another chair, staring sleepily at an old French movie. He wore hardware in a shoulder rig.

The man in black came up quietly from the rear and opened wide those sleepy eyes with a nylon necktie that buried itself in that soft flesh at the throat.

The guard stiffened and threshed around a bit before slumping into final rest but the one on the couch was not at all disturbed. Bolan walked past that one and pushed open the bedroom door. A rather large, distinguished-looking man in pajamas sat propped on pillows on the bed, reading by a bed lamp.

The guy raised his eyes to stare calmly at the intruder, and he was still staring without comment when the Beretta put a sighing round between those eyes.

Bolan closed that door and returned to give the sleeper one of the same, then he crossed to the connecting door to the adjoining suite and entered firing.

The first round caught a hawk-nosed skinny torpedo who was digging for a Coke in an ice chest. The next found a wild-eyed little guy in underwear who'd just stepped from the bathroom and tried too late to change his mind. Two other guys, obviously torpedoes, came running in from the other room. Both had apparently been preparing for bed and were partially disrobed, though each still wore a hardware rig and each was trying to get clear of the other in order to launch an effective response. For a panicky microsecond, there, they seemed to be fighting each other—then Bolan resolved that mini-conflict with a Parabellum snorter for each. One of the recipients was unfortunate enough to have caught his a trifle low; the hollownose slug tore in just beneath the chin and popped the guy back through the doorway. He was lying back there whistling through his open throat when Bolan sent him another to the proper place.

It was one of those small, off-number errors which could one day write *finis* to a perfectionist such as Mack Bolan.

The noise-suppressor for the Beretta was Bolan's very own—devised and built by the man himself—and it was really quite effective. The reports through that silencer were hardly more than a faintly whistling sigh—a soft *chooong* sound—but it was an audible sound, and it could be heard, especially in confined areas.

Add to that the thump of a heavy body going down under a sloppy hit—and, yeah, a guy behind enemy lines could be in trouble.

Bolan thought for sure he was, when the other four from the final suite came charging in to investigate. There were oohs and aahs and Italian exclamations, and then there were people flinging themselves off into four directions at once and handguns booming—and, hell, that kind of racket was the last thing Bolan had wanted.

A reload for the Beretta was not part of the problem, requiring no more than one second flat to eject the spent clip and chuck in another. But some sensing of the combat mind had already sprung Big Thunder into that strong right hand and—with the fat already in the fire—there was no reluctance to give the big piece its thundering head.

The first sizzling round of .44 magnum caught a guy whirling across toward the window and sent him sprawling head first through the glass and on out the window.

The second, coming like an immediate echo, grabbed another guy by the throat and set him spinning like a dervish with blood spurting everywhere.

A guy on the floor, just under that, jackknifed away in perfect timing to collect the next big 240-grain bullet in the ear—and the fourth man of the set took his through the upholstered seat of an overturned chair, dead center between the eyes.

Heavy feet were pounding along the hallway and the rising sounds of excited voices were making themselves heard from above and below when Bolan slipped back into the shaft and secured the panel in place.

And, sure, he'd lost his numbers—on the very first hit. Room phones or no, the entire joint would be at battle stations within the next few minutes.

The "quiet initiative" would have no chance, now.

The soft war was over—nearly as soon as it had begun.

He was resolved, however, to make as much hay as his waning sun would allow.

The Executioner was climbing fast and furious, headed for the farthest point possible from that zone of alarm.

He would hit the fifteenth floor, and all he could reach there. The penthouse would of course be directly overhead, and most of Joe Staccio's outraged force was probably up there right now.

So okay.

Let hell claim its own.

The Executioner was blitzing.

Larry Attica took a nervous pull at his cigarette and declared: "I don't like it, Mr. Turrin. It just ain't natural for all the phones to just go out like that. I mean, *all* of them?"

"You been in Manhattan lately?" Turrin growled. "You can spend half your time without phones in that town. Relax, Larry. They're just replacing some equipment in the central exchange. We'll be back in by morning."

"I still don't like it," Attica insisted.

"You don't have to like it," the underboss said. "You just have to live with it. Did you get your people deployed?"

The crew chief from Syracuse ground out his cigarette and lit another as he replied, "Yessir. I got them on two-section watch—four hours on and four off. Now I put two boys on each floor. One is at the elevators. The other is patrolling the hall. I got ten down in the lobby and another four at the side entrance. Outside, I got one boy watching each side of the building—down on the ground—and I put one on each wall, up here on the roof. Now if the guy can come through all that, then by God he's some kind of ghost."

"Yeah, it sounds good and tight," Turrin agreed.

"I just wish we had phones. If I knew where to get them, I'd send out for a crate full of walkie-talkies. I don't like this damn communications gap."

The underboss from Pittsfield chuckled and told the worrier from Syracuse: "You got it under control, Larry—stop worrying. The men in

New York are going to be hearing some nice things about you, after this. Believe me."

Attica puffed noticeably under that praise. "Like you said, Mr. Turrin—somebody had to take hold. I'm sorry about Joe—I mean, I feel like pulling my hair and yelling every time I think about that—but, God, the world didn't come to an end with Joe Staccio. I mean, this is the meet of the century. It would be terrible, just terrible, if this thing fell all to hell now."

"Augie would be very unhappy about that," Turrin solemnly agreed. "Don't you worry none, he's going to appreciate and remember the way you boys closed in behind Joe and held the thing together. What's Little Al doing, by the way?"

Attica jerked his head toward the bedroom. "He's sitting with the body. Got 'im on ice, in the bathtub."

"That's a terrible thing," Turrin said. He got to his feet and strolled to the window. Terrible, sure—but the world sometimes was a terrible place. Joe Staccio had simply collected his own due. The guy had certainly added more than his share of terror to the world. Guys like Staccio deserved no dignity in death. Life, to them, was profane—nothing but a four-letter word. Could their own deaths be anything more?

Attica called over, "I wonder what Mr. Ruggi is doing."

"He's very busy," Turrin replied in a muffled voice. Yeah, sure, Mr. Ruggi must be very busy at this very moment. Turrin wheeled away from that window and took two steps toward the center of the room when the booming report of distant guns momentarily froze him to the spot. His gaze locked with Attica's alarmed leap of eyes and both men made a fast break toward the terrace.

Electrified men were moving energetically about that roof.

Attica yelled, "What is it?"

The sentry at the south wall cupped his hands to call back, "Gunfire below! Someone just fell through a window, down there! Third or fourth floor!"

"Aw *shit!*" Attica agonized. He ran back into the apartment, where the off-duty security force was quickly grouping. "Half of you to the third floor, half to the fourth!" he yelled. "Know who you're shooting at, but don't take no shit offa nobody!"

Leo Turrin ambled on to the south parapet where he joined the sentry in a cautious observation of the situation below. The gunfire had ended. Indeed—it had come and gone so quickly that a guy could even wonder if his ears had been playing tricks. Turrin knew better than that, though.

Mr. Ruggi was indeed very busy.

And Leo Turrin was even more worried than Worrying Larry Attica. Something more important than the Montreal Meet was at stake here.

Something had evidently gone wrong down there—and a noble life had just committed itself to a battle line—not a profane life, not a four-letter-word life, but a magnificently superb one.

And, sure, Leo Turrin was a worried man.

"Hang in there, guy," he muttered to himself.

"Sir?" asked the parapet guard.

Turrin looked at the guy, and actually saw him for the first time. Hardly more than a kid, early twenties—probably a Vietnam vet with nothing in his bag of life but guns, bucks, and broads.

"I said it's a lousy life," Turrin replied.

The kid grinned engagingly and told the under-boss from Pittsfield, "Just let me get a shot at that bastard, sir, and you won't hear me complaining."

Turrin smiled and walked away.

True, kid, true. Get close enough to Mack Bolan to take a shot at him—and nothing in the whole world would be close enough to hear your final complaint.

The world wasn't lousy—it was just savage.

And Leo Turrin was placing his chips on the largest savage of them all.

17: HONORS

The thought had not occurred to Larry Attica
that he might die. That was not the worry. The
thing so in control of his emotions at this moment
was the fear of failure. A third-ranker with a
small-town territory did not every day get a shot
at the top. The developments in Montreal had
come as a gift from heaven—success on a plat-
ter—and maybe the one big moment of his life.

A guy had to seize those moments. He had to
make them pay. And Larry Attica certainly intended to make this one pay. With Staccio out of
the picture and the whole upstate territory open to
bids, the man from Syracuse could just see himself going into the game with a pat hand. The
great, burdening fear now was that the whole
thing was falling apart under him—that he

would leave Montreal in disgrace, not in triumph.

He wanted so much to be introduced to Augie Marinello as "the boy who saved the Montreal Meet." God! Imagine that! And if it could also be said, "This is the boy who brought in Bolan the Bastard's head"—sweet Jesus!—who or what could stand in Larry Attica's path to the top after that?

Guys like Frank Ruggi would stand in line to shake Larry Attica's hand.

Guys like Leo the Pussy Turrin would have to step back and make room for another candidate to the Council of Kings while those tired old men like Augie Marinello found a new favorite to lean on.

Hell, there was no end to it!

Larry Attica was on a skyrocket ride to the top!

He was going to pull it off, too. If that guy Bolan had really come back—if he was really dumb enough to try them again, now that the hard was on, then by God Larry Attica was going to have Mack Bolan's balls!

The fear, however, remained. So much was at stake. And it was this fear, this trembling realization of *moment*, which perhaps tipped the scales of destiny and sent Larry Attica down the stairs with a handpicked crew instead of into the elevators with the main force.

He simply had to play all possibilities. The idea

was to spot-check each floor on the way down to the trouble area.

And, yes, it proved to be an inspired idea.

It had required perhaps two minutes from the first sound of gunfire below until the Attica counterforce was organized and crowding into the elevators. Georgie Corona and Sam Paoli remained behind with Attica, then followed him down the stairwell for the "floor shake."

He explained the procedure as they hurried down the first flight of stairs. "We'll use the boys on floor duty to help shake it. I'll stick at the stairway door, that'll leave four of you to run along those halls and hit every door. Don't waste time with explanations. Just hit the door and check to see that everything's okay inside."

"Some of these guys don't speak English," Corona panted. "How do we—"

"I said don't waste time. If you get an answer, any answer, it's okay."

They burst through the stairway door at the fifteenth level, and the floormen there immediately came running.

"Door check!" Attica called to them. He gave his other two boys a push as he yelled, "You got a minute! Make it quick!"

The checkers ran off in two-man teams, beginning at the middle and working toward the ends, a man to each side of the hall—banging doors and yelling, "Security check!"

Attica nervously lit a cigarette and maintained

137

a tense vigil at the midpoint—shouting reassur-
ances at the startled men who'd come to their
doors to find nothing there but pyramiding confusion.

He kept yelling, "It's okay, go back inside—
routine check!"

Apparently there did exist a communications
problem, however. Excited voices were raised in
several languages all along that hallway—and no
one seemed to understand what was happening.

A bald-headed guy in a bathrobe must have decided that the building was on fire, and was
loudly wondering, in strongly accented French, as
to the whereabouts of the fire escape. *"Où estl'escalier de secours? Ay? Ay? L'escalier?"*

Attica was yelling, "No, no, it's okay! Go back
to bed! Routine—" when a door halfway along
the east side banged open and a guy came
backpedaling out of there with a gun in his hand
and blasting like crazy at something inside the
room.

The crew chief from Syracuse had already begun regretting his hasty approach to the security
check—he'd only panicked the whole damn floor
and now here was a guy going crazy with a gun.
Before that idea was wholly formed in Attica's
reeling mind, however, another one leapt in to re-
place it—and this one needed no time for formation. The head of that crazy guy down there
suddenly went off in several directions at once—
flinging parts of itself in a spray onto the wall

like an overripe melon falling from a truck. And even before that body could hit the deck, another came sliding out of the same room with a gun in its hand and a gushing hole where its nose had been.

With all that to occupy his mind, Attica was still able to appreciate the sudden silence in that hallway and to reflect for perhaps one heartbeat upon the effect of gunfire on a panicky crowd.

Every man Jack in that hall was packing hardware, most of them waving their guns around like cheerleaders with pompons.

Two dead men were lying in their own fluids on that hallway floor. Twenty or thirty guys with guns in their hands were just standing there gawking at the mess. Only Georgie Corona and Sam Paoli seemed to have any presence of mind. They were returning from the opposite end of the building, shoving people back through their open doorways and clearing that hall as rapidly as possible.

Elapsed time from the first bloodspray: perhaps ten seconds. Attica himself had just found his own voice, calling to the floormen on the east end: "Watch it, boys, watch it. We got something here."

The "guests" on that end were getting the idea also. They were quietly easing back to their rooms and peering through cracked doors to cautiously evaluate the situation.

The floormen had reached the death scene and

were tentatively poking at the bodies with their feet. One of them called to Attica: "I see another one inside, boss. Just like these."

Georgie and Sam joined their boss at the midpoint as Attica was calling instructions to the other tow: "Leave 'em be. Stay right there but get back away from that door."

Elapsed time: about twenty seconds.

Corona said, "It couldn't be, could it?"

"Sure it could," Attica snarled.

"Clear from the third floor?"

"Don't ask how, dammit. If he's here, he's here—and we want to keep it that way. Get those two boys into the rooms next door. They watch that window, understand? Anything trying to come through it gets sieved. Understand? Then you and Sam take 'im through the front. I'll stick here and backdrop the whole thing."

Corona and Paoli exchanged uneasy glances, then moved on to the combat zone.

The floormen split up and entered the rooms to either side of the death room.

The other two hardmen took positions outside the door, pistols up and ready. Paoli slipped inside, then Corona. At that precise moment, the door directly opposite opened and something fell to the floor of the hallway—a small stick-like object. Attica's mind leapt at that object and simultaneously the object leapt at Attica, sending a dense black cloud spiraling along the hallway.

Smoke!

The crew boss screamed a warning to his hard-men and flung himself back along the wall in a quick retreat while his thought processes strained at the impossibility of one guy being two places at one moment.

So this was how the guy got his reputation.

No wonder hardened veterans of the savage streets turned tail and ran from a guy like that. He was just too stunning, too tricky, *too damned deadly*—and Larry Attica, the ambitious third-ranker from Syracuse, was very suddenly running out of ambition.

He was also running out of people.

Sam Paoli was the first to fall clear of that burgeoning smoke screen, and he came out of there as though shot from a gun. The truth was that he had been shot by a gun—one vicious hell of a gun, to judge by the hole in Sammy's head and by the force of the dive that kept him rolling along that floor like a ball off its string. A silenced gun with a chilling *choong* was its only voice. Then, dammit, it *choonged* again as a steel-wire voice somewhere back in there clearly stated in tones of mild regret: "Sorry, Georgie."

Sorry, Georgie—sure, that could mean only one thing—*no more Georgie*—and unambitious Larry Attica was headed for the stairway door, post-haste.

There was something about that voice—familiar but also unfamiliar—different but not different—*different from what?*

141

The fleeing crew boss snapped off two shots into the approaching smoke screen and stepped clear, into the stairwell. He had only a glimpse through the octagonal glass panel of the deadly dude in black who was moving along within that screen, the eyes protected by goggles, a big silver blaster in one hand and a bulb-tipped zinger in the other. The guy was firing both pieces at once, sending a withering fusillade along that hall and tearing into walls and doors with the crack of a dozen axes all going at once.

A few people at the other end were apparently sending back halfhearted responses but the guy moved on past the stairwell door without pause.

Larry Attica crossed himself and started up the stairs. In his haste, he lost his footing and fell forward onto the steps. His pistol accidentally discharged to send a bullet ricocheting around the steel stairwell as he raised himself to all fours and scampered on to the safety of numbers upstairs. Then the thought crashed into his mind that he had sent all the boys below—all but the roofmen and Little Al.

There was comfort enough in those numbers, however, and he was reaching for it with everything he had when that door down there crashed open and a puff of smoke entered the stairwell.

That was not, of course, all that entered.

The guy was there, looking up at him over those smoking guns. The goggles were now riding

142

the forehead and those unmasked eyes were giving Larry Attica the requiem gaze.

The crew master from Syracuse was too stunned to even lift his gun. *"You!"* he croaked in a shocked whisper, and that was his last word.

"Sorry, Larry," said the man in black, and then that big silver pistol belched like a blowhole from hell and sent Larry Attica's skyrocket to lift him to his final honor.

It carried him up a couple of steps, then over the rail in a plunge to the depths—as some skyrockets are wont to do.

"You earned this, guy," the man in black said solemnly as he flipped a marksman's medal into the wake of that plunging body.

Yeah. It was the final honor for a hardworking torpedo: the Unholy Order of *Corpus Delicti*.

It was an honor that he would share with many, on this night of nights.

The Montreal Meet would convene in hell.

18:   SIX PACK

It was obvious to Leo Turrin that the whole joint was going to hell in a hurry.

Two guys, in the last few minutes, had jumped from high windows and another half-dozen or so had been shot off of fire escapes. Smoke was pouring out of windows from the twelfth floor to the fifteenth. Obviously someone had turned in a fire alarm—sirens were screaming in from all directions and the streets down there were rapidly filling with people.

The guys on the roof were getting edgy as hell—and with good reason. It could be a bad place to be, with the joint on fire.

Turrin found the roof chief and told him, "Use your own head, guy. Take your boys off of here any time you think it's right."

"Are you leaving, Mr. Turrin?" the guy wanted to know.

"Yeah. I got to go see what's happening down there."

The roof chief pulled at his chin as he thought it over. "I guess we can hang loose awhile longer. Mr. Attica said stay. We'll stay as long as we can."

Turrin gave the guy an encouraging squeeze on the shoulder and went on toward the apartment. He found a dark spot on the terrance and stepped into it, dug a small transistor radio from his pocket, popped in a miniature earphone, and pushed the call button.

Hal Brognola's agitated tones leapt right back at him. "I was beginning to think you'd never speak. What the hell is that guy doing? There was nothing said about torching the joint."

Turrin replied, "I think he's just making smoke. Where are you?"

"Right under you. I can't control this situation much longer, pal. They're wanting to come in."

"Hold them as long as possible," Turrin requested. "Tell them anything but give them nothing."

Brognola growled back, "That's easy to say from where you're standing. Okay. I'll twist all the arms I can."

Turrin put the radio away and went inside.

Al DeCristi jumped out from behind a drapery with a snarling challenge. "What the hell are you doing, Turrin?"

He looked the guy up and down and told him "That's *Mister* Turrin to you, DeCristi. What's the matter with you?"

"You was using a radio. I saw you."

"Go suck a fart, guy," Turrin coldly replied. "I'll use a TV and a string band if I get the notion, and I won't be coming to you for permission."

He walked on, ignoring the pistol in the little bodyguard's hand. The guy had tipped his rocker, that was sure—but Turrin knew how to handle a guy like that.

Maybe.

"Mr. Turrin!"

He halted and turned a profile to the guy. "Yeah?"

"The hotel is burning."

"Thanks for the news. I'll give it first spot on my next radio broadcast."

"What do I do with *him*?"

Meaning, of course, the remains of Jumping Joe Staccio.

"You mean *it*," Turrin replied cruelly. "Don't lose your head over a stiff, Al. Get out of here. Joe don't need you anymore."

He went on, through the glass doors and into the vestibule. He tossed a quick look over his shoulder as he exited, but there was no sign of the little guy.

Turrin shook his head and then dismissed the whole thing from his mind. He debated briefly be-

tween the elevator and the stairs and quickly decided in favor of the hard way, deciding that it
was probably the only way.

He entered the stairwell to pandemonium. Fast
feet and excited talk rose up to him from every
level as alarmed men moved energetically along
that exit.

The panic was in and the rout was on.

Leo Turrin had been a first-hand observer on
many a scene such as this. It seemed that when
Mack Bolan moved, the whole world moved with
him—or away from him.

Not a bad idea, at that.

The guy was mean enough when his situation
was merely untenable. When it became impossible, Mack Bolan became downright formidable—and, yeah, even "the impossible" moved over
and made room for Mr. Blitz.

It required a full five minutes for Turrin to
make his way from the penthouse to the fifth
floor—and the going became tougher with each
level passed. Guys were pushing and cussing each
other in the wild scramble to quit that turf—and
Leo himself had to backhand a couple of Euro-
peans who were showing too little respect for his
place on the stairway.

The smoke was puffing through as low as the
eighth-floor level by the time Turrin passed that
point, so he knew that the big guy was still plying
his trade and fanning the flames of panic. The
underboss from Pittsfield did not exactly under-

stand the rationale of that but he'd quit arguing with Bolan's tactics long ago. The guy knew what he was doing and—bet on it—he was doing it all towards a coldly calculated effect.

Turrin had to knee a guy to get through that fifth-floor doorway. He was definitely bucking the flow of traffic but if things seemed bad here, he was trying to visualize the crush-effect down in the lobby ... with all exits barred and the streets outside knee-deep in Montreal cops.

He finally got it into the suite shared with "Ruggi" and lost no time cranking into the hot-line to Ottawa.

One of Brognola's agents took the call.

"What's the situation there, Pointer?" the guy asked with no social preamble whatever.

"Very tense," Leo the Pointer Turrin told the guy from Justice Washington. "Your boss is down in the street trying to hold back the dam of outraged police ethics. I think it's a losing battle, though, and the dam is liable to break at any moment. Meanwhile, out in the lake, the fishes are biting at everything. Striker has them falling over each other's asses and even trying to climb up them. The rout is definitely on but I'd say we need, at the inside, another half hour to realize a clean sweep. What's the word from the other side?"

"Grim," was the one-word response.

"You'd better give it to me."

The man from Washington sent a harsh sigh

along that hotline. "The decision came down an hour ago from the PM's office. Ottawa will cooperate fully."

"So what's grim?" Turrin growled.

"Grim is the confrontation now shaping up between Ottawa and Montreal. I understand that the leaders of *Parti Quebeçois* are in emergency caucus at this very moment. Their radicals apparently view the entire thing as a conspiracy to violate Quebec's sovereignty. As of this moment, the PM does not have any emergency powers to throw at them, but—"

"I didn't think the provinces had sovereignty," Turrin said.

"Maybe it depends on the point of view. It isn't so much a legal question, anyway—it's a political one—and that's been a hot area between Ottawa and Montreal for some time, or hadn't you noticed."

"Give me the bottom line," Turrin said, sighing.

"Ottawa is backing down. Wavering, anyway. It is entirely a police matter, some advisers are now saying, and therefore entirely within the jurisdiction of Montreal to handle."

"Sure," growled the man from Pittsfield. "This is crazy, Bender, and you know it. You call it politics, I'll call it the international clout machine. This whole damn town is liable to go up in flames before morning. Whose jurisdiction will it be then?"

"Hey, look, man—calm down. *I* can't send Her Majesty's troops into that province. Nobody can do that but—"

Turrin growled, "Yeah, yeah!" and flung the phone down.

He turned around just in time to see the Man from Blood step through the wall.

The guy looked like twenty hells.

He smelled of gunpowder and spent human blood and he bore liberally the telltale marks of both. He'd taken a minor graze wound at the left shoulder and another beneath the ribs. Ammo pockets on the belts as well as utility pouches everywhere gaped empty and useless. He was favoring the left leg and moving slower than Leo Turrin had ever noted as he moved on into the room.

Bolan went straight to the bathroom, drew a glass of water, and slowly downed it before acknowledging the presence of his old buddy and fellow survivor of many such campaigns.

"What's the lie, Leo?" he quietly inquired.

"Panic in the anthill," Turrin reported soberly. "What's yours?"

"Fatigue in the bones and combat weary all over the body. What's happening?"

The little guy from the knife's edge wet a washcloth and began dabbing at his friend's scratches. "It's hard to say what's happening," he replied. "General consensus has the building on fire. Human nature has several hundred bodies swarming the stairways and piling up in the lobbies, scratching for a way out. A thousand cops are on the street and two or three fire companies are adding to the general confusion. Ottawa says Montreal is in an emergency situation while Montreal says that Ottawa should stick the queen up their ass. I don't know what the hell is happening, Sarge. Maybe you better tell me."

Bolan pushed the fussing ministrations away and told the nation's top undercover cop: "Scratch Naples. Scratch Zurich. Ditto Berlin and Frankfurt with a question mark for Marseilles and Paris. I split the delegation from Brazil and I took a couple from Tokyo. Beyond that, hell, I don't know. The thing just got too wild. How do you call shots in a stampede?"

"How many rounds were you carrying, Sarge?" the little guy quietly inquired.

"Six clips of thunder, six of whisper," Bolan replied matter-of-factly, the voice practically a monotone.

Turrin did a quick interpolation and winced with the result. The guy was a phenomenal marksman and a genuine miser with combat rounds. A round spent was usually a life spent, as well.

"Was that you, plunking at the fire escapes?" he asked quietly.

"That's where I caught the crew from Brazil," the warrior said. He went to the closet and tiredly dragged out a suitcase, opened it, and began replenishing for his war effort.

Turrin watched in disbelief for a quiet moment, then inquired, "Now what the hell are you doing?"

"Blitzing," was the simple reply.

"That's what you *did*, buddy. What you're doing now is *withdrawing*. Quick and clean. Leave the rest for the scavenger crews."

"The clout machine is too strong here for that and you know it," the big guy declared matter-of-factly. "They're foreign nationals. The harshest thing they might get is an order to leave the country. And they'll laugh all the way home. Once they've settled their nerves, the same clowns will be back with the same hungry plans. If not here, somewhere else. I'm not going to give them that, Leo."

"There's too damned many, Sarge." Turrin was pleading, now. "You can't carry that many bullets."

The big tired guy in black showed his friend a tight smile and told him, "Relax, guy—I haven't slipped off the edge. I know what I'm doing."

"Well how 'bout letting me know."

The smile stayed. "How many cops did you say are down there?"

"Hell, it looks like a thousand. Probably a hundred or so, anyway. Why?"

"Cops in Montreal carry guns, don't they?"

"Sure. They got a hell of an impressive—"

"They'll shoot back if they're shot at, won't they? Even if a foreign national is involved?"

152

"Hey! Hey, now."

"It's a modern force? They have the usual protections? Look, Leo, I'm not trying to get a bunch of cops killed. But I'm betting that most of those guys out there know exactly who is overflowing this building. I'm betting they'd like nothing better than to slap down hard on some foreign crud who came here to eat their town. All they need is an excuse. Right?"

"And you're going to give it to them."

"No. The boys themselves are going to give it to them. I'm just going to push a little, from the rear."

"With six clips of thunder and six of whisper, eh?"

Bolan stood up and double-checked his belts. "It's a double six-pack, yeah. But the whisper is off. It's all thunder, now."

Turrin sighed and went to the door. "You're a lunatic, guy," he said quietly. "But give the boys a six-pack for Leo, huh?"

The Bolan grin spread just a fraction, but all the tired was still there. "I'll do that. Where will you be, Leo?"

"On the roof. I wouldn't miss this show for a ringside seat at the mating between a donkey and an orangutan."

The big guy was still grinning at him as he stepped into the hall and pulled the door shut.

What a hell of a guy. A push from the rear, huh? Okay, sure, it could work. If Hal could hold the cops on their line and keep the pressure at the front, and if Bolan could put just a little more heat on that pressure burner at the rear—then yeah, sure, the boys could decide to try shooting their way out.

It would, after all, be their only option.

The Sarge was running a force play.

And he was running it with *formidable* force. Right up their trembling asses.

19: TWENTY QUESTIONS, ONE ANSWER

Bolan was satisfied that Leo Turrin was in the clear now. Whatever else may occur during this night of nights, the little big guy's cover should remain intact—at least, insofar as the association with "Frank Ruggi" could have compromised it. Even if there remained a few who could infer some unwholesome association between the two, it seemed highly unlikely that any direct line could be drawn between "Ruggi" and Mack Bolan.

So he was leaving Leo to his own artifices and devices. And, of course, it always came down to that. The two stood isolated and alone most of the time, with their lives and diverging roles occasionally coming together for a brief touching—

then it was back to solitary for the both of them, each for himself and standing alone.

Now, Bolan was preparing to quit that place for once and all. He wiped down all possible fingerprint surfaces and removed every possible item which could conceivably link Mack Bolan to Frank Ruggi. He would push his farewell blitz of the lower levels and break clear via Montreal underground, regain his battle cruiser, and head for open country.

Or so he thought.

He was standing at room center and making a final visual sweep of the premises when the wall opened and a machine gun's snout poked into the room.

The .44 hit his hand and hung there in the firing lineup, stayed by some subliminal recognition of the unfamiliar figure which stepped out behind that impressive weapon.

The visitor was Betsy Gordon. She was rigged up in neo-American guerilla garb of black jumpsuit and swagger hat, crossed gunbelts, wicked autopistol hanging from the shoulders in a cross-chest carry—and her purposes did not appear friendly.

"You *bastard!*" she snarled at the tired man in black.

The AutoMag was looking at the emblem on her swagger hat—a bolt of lightning separating the letters Q and F, set in an open cluster of thorns.

Bolan looked her coolly up and down, then he thumbed-off his weapon and sheathed it. His voice was ice-water cold as he asked her, "Come for my blood, kid—or just to look at me?"

"I'm looking, Bolan," she assured him in matching tones. "And I don't like a damned thing I see."

"Move aside, Betsy. I've no time to jaw."

The muzzle of the burper moved ever so slightly and a quick burst ripped out of there, chewing a line across the floor an inch from his toes. "You want to try for ankles?" she promised, shaking rage building inside that voice.

Bolan knew the emotion. It was the kind that fed on itself. It was not one to be treated lightly.

He sighed and showed her the palms of his hands. "Put it down, kid. I've no fight with you. What's your squawk?"

"You told me to look," she said nastily. "Okay, I'm looking. Not at mirrors, either, Mr. Righteous. I see a pig—a rat—and a fink, all rolled into one Hollywood package. I'm going to shoot your legs off, Mr. America. Then we'll see how fast you can hobble back across the border on your rotten stumps!"

He chuckled quietly and told her, "Hell, I believe you're mad at me. When the women in Vietnam get mad at their men, they catch them asleep with a knife at their genitals."

"Don't give me ideas," she spat. "And whoever said you were my man!"

He was still chuckling, relaxing, allowing taut muscles to flow loose and pull him toward an at-ease position. One foot went back as he languidly turned away from that confrontation—and suddenly he was on her, one hand in control of that chatterpistol, the other at the girl's throat, his own towering frame bending her backward in a spine-threatening curl.

Angry fingers dug at him and panicky knees stretched toward his groin without success—then suddenly the fight was over as she let go with a moan.

Bolan hung onto the autopistol while allowing her to slide free. He removed the clip and pocketed it, placed the weapon on a chair, lifted the girl into his arms and carried her to the bed. Then he wet a towel and sponged that pretty face until she came around.

She lay passive though glaring up at him—most of the fight gone but glowing embers remaining to remind him of the wrath he'd faced.

"What's it all about, kid?" he asked quietly.

"Betrayal," she said, putting it all into one word.

"I haven't betrayed you, Betsy."

"What do you call it, then? You came to us as a friend, seeking support for your cause. We gave it gladly, because you lied to us."

He shook his head. "I did not lie to you."

"You said a quiet night, then homeward bound. You did not say open warfare, police thronging in

158

the streets, bayonets from Ottawa, destruction of our base."

Bolan stared at her for a tense moment, then he went over and collected the autopistol, fed in the clip, chambered a round, and returned to the bed. He placed the weapon on the bed beside the girl and told her, "Okay, this is the second time in the past twenty-four hours I've given one of you people a gun to hold at my head. If you can read dishonesty in that, then you go ahead and chop me down."

She had not made a move toward that weapon. The gazes clashed, then mingled—and then "the kid" came back home.

He sat beside her and gathered her in his arms, and he kissed her—but the kiss he received in return was that of a woman, not of a kid.

She cried a little and he comforted her a little. When the emotional moment was spent, she whispered to him, "Somehow I knew from the beginning that it was going to be like this. I want to make love, not war."

"There's a time for both," he said, sighing. He pushed away from that tender trap. "Right now, I'm afraid it's war."

"Let's say to hell with it. Right now. Let's go away and never look back."

"Is it that easy?" he asked quietly, looking away from those eyes.

"It's so confusing," she wailed. "I never know what to believe anymore."

"It's that kind of world," he muttered. "Too many questions, not enough answers. I'm sorry if I've caused your people any suffering. Please believe that nothing like that was intended. If it's any comfort, this building is not burning and I can't believe that I've betrayed any of its secrets. Just the same—I have to be honest about this—I'd rather see it burn. I think I understand the QF plans for this hotel. It's a bad strategy, Betsy. It will turn on you, and eat you."

Apparently he had revived her political spirit—with a challenge, as it were. She sat up and glowered at him, then the anger wavered and the eyes dropped.

"That damned mirror again?" he asked her.

"Maybe so," she replied miserably.

"Betsy. Understand something. I am not a terrorist. I do not cruise through Central Park spraying civilians with machine-gun fire as a protest to crime in the streets. I am a soldier fighting soldiers. My war *is* a war, in every sense of the word. Is yours?"

"We think so."

"With banners unfurled, drums and fifes, glory and hallelujah?" He shook his head. "Uh uh. You looked at me, earlier today, and you saw a mirror image reflecting back at you. You accused me of murder while actually accusing yourself. This building—" He spread his arms in an encompassing gesture. "This entire bizarre network, this *tree* of Montreal. Is it for war? Or is it for terrorist activity? Are you going to battle the soldiers of the crown here?"

She said, defensively, "If need be."

"No," he told her. "That is not the objective, and there is no confusion in your mind on that point. Like Bosquet said, it is magnificent but it is not war. It's a proxy war. You cannot take on the soldiers of the crown and you know it. So you substitute. You set up a straw enemy whom you can pummel at will, with no real contest involved. You attack the non-enemy, Betsy, because it's more comfortable that way."

"When the cause is right," she argued weakly, "a certain suffering is acceptable."

"Sure, but whose suffering—and acceptable to whom? That's the basic flaw in terrorist causes, Betsy. There's nothing noble or holy or even human about sacrificing innocent victims who have no voice in your cause, no reward in your victory. It's a proxy war, and I can't respect it. Neither can you. That's what's eating you. It's what causes your confusion, the endless examination of questions, the avoidance of final answers."

"We have all faced the decision to die," the girl murmured.

"So that makes it holy. That's a cop-out. The moment of decision comes when you're looking down the wrong end of a hostile gun. Why not do as the Buddhists do? Leave the holy rites to the holy men, and spare the innocent masses. Form a circle in the town square, douse each other with gasoline, and strike a match. I'll respect that, kid. But not this. You've been getting ready for the Olympic Games, haven't you, just like everybody else in Montreal? Just like this hotel has been preparing to house the honored guests from around the world. Isn't it ironic that the hoodlums came in first? Your tree house is perfect for my sort of war, *Quebeçoise*. But it's a pretty dismal approach to yours."

The girl was eyeing the machine pistol, as though maybe she was going to pick it up and start spraying again after all.

"Isn't it?" he prodded her.

"Brave men, brave women," she whispered. "Machine guns and hand grenades—against . . ."

"It needs rethinking," Bolan told her. "Nothing good and lasting can grow from soil like that."

"I guess you're right," she said quietly.

"Meanwhile, I've got this real war on my hands, Betsy. Bug off, huh?"

She gave him a shallow smile. "I'll try to convince my friends that what you say is true. But I promise nothing. They intend to cow the world, to bring international pressure to bear, to force political concessions for a free Quebec. That's a rather heady dream. I doubt that one voice will be heard in the clamor of that dream." She sighed. "But I will try."

"You could be surprised," Bolan told her as he tested his combat rig. "There could be other voices, just waiting for a strong one to rally around." He showed her a sudden grin. "You have a pretty strong voice, lady. I was seeing the end of *my* war a few minutes ago."

She dropped those fabulous eyes and murmured, "Sorry about that. And isn't this all so ridiculous? There you stand, armed for war, lecturing on peaceful solutions."

"It's a crazy world," he told her.

"I guess so."

Crazy had not yet, however, reached its full meaning. It approached that point one heartbeat later when Andre Chebleu and two others, togged out identically with the Gordon girl, stepped quickly through the wall.

The Executioner and the triple agent regarded each other through a quiet moment of mutual inspection—and it was the triple agent who broke the silence.

"You must leave at once," he announced, the voice taut but friendly. "Your moment has passed, here."

"Not quite," Bolan advised him. "A small matter remains, five floors below."

"You cannot move in that direction," Chebleu insisted. "The underground army is massing in the tunnels."

"Which army is this, now?" Bolan inquired.

"It is not QF," the Frenchman assured him, "but the storm troops of the new Mafia republic."

"Who leads them?"

Georgette's brother smiled at the Executioner.

"LeBlanc leads them—also known as Chebleu. Your moment has passed. Mine has arrived. Leave me to mine, *ami*."

Bolan had already made his decision. He nodded at the new hope for Quebec and told him, "It's all yours, *Quebeçois*."

Betsy Gordon scrambled off the bed, breathlessly making some inquiry in rapid-fire French. Chebleu gave her a quick reply in the same language—and Bolan caught a bit of that. Apparently Chebleu had enlisted the majority of QF in response to a new, more urgent cause.

The girl snatched up her autopistol and told Bolan, *"M'oui!* Your answer is now my answer. My war has arrived, *L'Exécuteur*."

Chebleu's pained gaze met Bolan's. A question and a returning answer crackled along the line of sight.

"She is a good soldier," Chebleu told his friend. "Will you accept her as my personal guarantee to you of safe passage to your border?"

Bolan's gaze shifted from the guy to the girl as he replied. He knew what Chebleu was asking. He did not want that girl in the tunnels. "She would probably be better off with you, Andre. But, yes, I may need a reliable flanker. If you can spare her, I'll take her part of the way."

The little guerilla was obviously torn between two desires. "But I—I . . ."

"You have an optional line of retreat, I assume," the Frenchman said to the Executioner.

"Always," Bolan replied with a surface smile.

The girl cried, "Well, wait! I—"

"You have your answer," Chebleu clipped at her. "You will protect our friend's withdrawal."

Chebleu and his shadows disappeared within the tree, leaving Bolan and the lady to contemplate the new relationship so skillfully thrust upon them.

There were, also, other considerations crowding the combat mind.

And yeah, sure, Bolan always had an alternate route of retreat. Even if, sometimes, that route had to be carved from raw territory.

He took his flanker by the arm and told her, "Prep your weapons. Get it all together. The final answer is waiting for us."

"And I," she said with a toss of the head, "am waiting for it."

She would, Bolan knew, find it very shortly.

20:   ALL TOGETHER

He sent Betsy Gordon to the top of the tree, to wait for him at the opening to the roof, while he took himself out the front door and along the hallway to the public stairway.

It was strangely quiet on the fifth level, with not a soul stirring but Bolan's own, and it remained so until he opened the door to that enclosed stairwell. Then the hubbub from below swelled up like lamentations from the crypt—and he knew that the boys were ready for a shot of inspiration in the rear.

The languages of the world were represented in that bawling from below—and although the words themselves were not clear, the sentiments were. Those guys down there were outraged, querulous, frightened, and defiant all at once.

Curses and obscenities universal to all languages floated freely in that frustrated atmosphere of containment and panic.

And, yeah, this was Mack Bolan's kind of war. This enemy was a rabble, sure, but a rabble of armed soldiers who'd committed misspent lives to the questions of violence and depravity but—like others—were not prepared to face the final answer. These guys could shoot back, if they would—yet none had probably ever faced up to his own final answer with anything other than a proxy enemy. That was one of the problems of the world: too damn many proxies, not enough true confrontations. A cop was a proxy. So was a judge, a congressman, a legislator, a preacher or priest or rabbi. Everybody, it seemed, wanted someone else to handle the important affairs of the world.

In a one-on-one situation, most men could handle their own problems with justice. But if the guy had to take the abuse from a savage, then call a cop as the first in a long line of stand-ins to represent him in exacting justice for the abuse— well, sure, it was easy to lose it all in the tangle.

If every savage in the world knew that each civilized man had the means and the will to retaliate immediately and effectively upon any trespass of his fundamental rights—then the days of human savagery would be numbered.

Mack Bolan believed that with all his understanding of brute psychology. It was, indeed, his own motivation. He was, in the final sense, a proxy himself. He was Judgment. He had come to Montreal to call the roll, and he'd come to this point of this night in Montreal to call it again—certain in his soul that all who heard would stampede away toward a more comfortable enemy.

He swiftly descended the stairway, shattering light bulbs with the butt of the AutoMag as he passed them, bringing darkness with him until he stood at the final flight above the bawling crowd.

The problem, down there, was obvious.

There was no more room at the inn.

That lobby was packed with frantic humanity, the forward edge all but crushed by the insistent packing from the rear—and still they were backed up into the stairwell and halfway up the first flight of stairs. Through the glass transom above the stairwell door, Bolan had an excellent view from the second-floor landing—across the herd and through the windows out front, onto the street. Police vehicles were out there en masse, including armored riot vehicles, paddy wagons, the whole smear. A PA system was blaring announcements in three languages, monotonously alternating the message of the night: REMAIN CALM. THERE IS NO DANGER. THIS BUILDING IS QUARANTINED.

Bolan had to grin at that. A quarantine, sure, against the deadliest disease of mankind: organized crime.

168

Those guys in the lobby were not buying that bit about "no danger." The place was on fire, wasn't it? The damn fire trucks were sitting out there, weren't they? A maniac was running wild somewhere in there, wasn't he, shooting people down, on sight, like wild dogs in the streets.

The sizing of the situation was accomplished with one flash of the combat eyes. The next flash sent thunder and lightning into that crowd on the stairs. A fat guy with a bald head was the first to lend himself to the accentuation of panic, flinging his life forces onto the surrounding crowd. A guy standing in the splatter zone was the next to go. He saw the apparition in black and raised a hand to ward off his call but the messenger splattered on through that flimsy shield and took the guy in the ear.

There was not even room down there for the victims to lie down in death. They hung in the crowd, grisly heads testifying to the "danger" in that place as those about them lunged and plunged to escape a similar fate.

The Man from Death stood calmly at that landing and continued the challenge, hurling word after thundering word into the howling pack, placing his rounds with care for maximum effect—through the transom, under it, around it. Handguns were exploding down there but their bullets had no sense of direction nor even any recognition between friend and foe.

The truth of the matter was that those guys down there had not a friend left in the world.

They were now a frenzied herd of animals stampeding in the face of death.

The windows at the front gave and the spillover into the street became a fact of the night. The animals were waving their weapons and shooting at anything—and the retort from the street, true to Bolan's guess, was immediate and withering.

He sheathed his weapons and withdrew.

The Montreal Meet would go down as the grisliest of memories for the international brotherhood of savages.

And Mack Bolan had no regrets in that regard, none whatever. He knew that as long as he lived, it would take a hell of lot of arm twisting to engineer another international meet.

He had no apologies at all to offer his victims.

"Let them eat themselves," he muttered, and made his way to the roof.

It was not over yet. A matter of tactical disengagement remained, and he was hoping that the option was still open.

She was waiting for him at the top of the shaft, a mere waif in a soldier's suit huddled on the little platform at the topmost branch of the tree.

"I was getting worried," she whispered. "The gunfire keeps getting louder and louder."

"That's coming from the street," he told her. "It's a perfect cover. Let's go."

Bolan led the way outside and held the trick door for his flanker. "Stay one pace behind and to my left," he quietly instructed her. "Fire at my command only and call your shots. Understand?"

The girl nodded her understanding of the instructions and moved into position.

Bolan stepped away from the wall and moved cautiously across the garden terrace, senses alert for some sign of Leo Turrin.

He found, first, Joe Staccio.

The body was laid out naked on the artifical lawn with a small mountain of ice cubes covering the body. His flanker gasped at the sight of that but there was no need to shush her.

Standing off about six paces, beside a potted tree, was Leo.

The muzzle of a Colt was at the back of his head, and behind the gun stood Little Al DeCristi.

It was one of those sudden confrontations, an eyeball meet from out of nowhere—and the moment congealed outside of space and time.

The entire world seemed encapsulated in that frozen moment. It finally, always, came down to a moment such as this—and Bolan had learned to expect them although there was simply no way in the world of space and time to prepare for them.

DeCristi began cackling like a crazy man.

Leo said, "Don't let him suck you, Sarge. Blow him out."

171

Translated: I'm a dead man anyway and so are you if you play his game.

Bolan knew the game.

And he knew guys like Little Al DeCristi. Faithful servants to the end, a life in the shadow of a life—the true meaning of fealty. For guys like DeCristi, Bolan had always felt a twinge of something approaching respect—even though they deserved it no more than a bird deserved respect for flying.

Bolan moved only his lips to instruct his flanker. "Put a burst into the ice," he commanded.

No sooner said than done. The hot little burper sent ice flying everywhere and the body beneath it quivered with the impact of steel-jacketed slugs at high velocity.

DeCristi's horrified attention flew there for one fatal instant—an instant outside of space and time—and then Leo Turrin was on the deck and rolling and the .44 was saying goodbye to fealty.

The hit flipped the little guy around like a rag doll and deposited him alongside ice mountain.

"Slick, slick," Turrin growled as he rolled to his feet. He cast a quick glance at the lady with the chattergun and the question was there in the eyes but there was no time to voice it.

Several boys were running over from the south wall, all that remained of the roof crew. They had been watching the massacre on the street, and it was a wonder that they even heard the rooftop gunfire in the background of all that. But they had, and they were coming to investigate.

Turrin told Bolan, "There's only three. That's one apiece. Let's take them."

"We'll take them," Bolan replied, indicating the girl with a flash of his eyes. "You get that chopper up here."

Turrin nodded and moved clear, digging into his pocket for the radio.

The Executioner's icy eyes gave his flanker a glint of confidence as he explained her fire assignment. "I'll be moving center and right. You take whatever pops on my left flank."

She was scared, sure, but it was the fear of the novice—the green soldier—more afraid of herself and her own reactions than of any enemy.

Bolan's fear was a professional one. He knew that all of life was lived on the heartbeat, and he knew how frail was that beat. One stagger, one moment of indecision or one heartbeat of error— no matter who the enemy—could mean the end of war.

The final answer, always, is death.

This girl had to learn that—if only in the way Bolan had.

He moved across the steps of the penthouse terrace and went down to meet the enemy, his petite flanker and apprentice-at-war moving quietly in his shadow.

These boys were playing it cagey. They'd split

173

up and were moving stealthily now along three converging lines of approach.

Bolan found his position and pushed the girl into the shadow of a potted tree. "Wait them to the wall," he whispered.

She nodded understanding and crouched over her weapon.

Bolan grinned at her and she smiled back, though it was a quick one.

The first one to show himself was in her fire zone. The guy slithered over the wall and was down in the shadow of it in a twinkling. Bolan saw it, and he saw Betsy's muzzle lunge toward that target but a heartbeat too late. She stayed her trigger finger and Bolan said to himself, *good girl.*

The other two followed almost immediately. First, one up over the right flank then another at dead center—the latter hefting a short shotgun and moving a bit less gracefully over that low wall.

Bolan hit the guy on the right with a thunder round as he was dropping toward the shadow. It was a sloppy hit. The guy fell with a gurgle and was thrashing around in the darkness. The second round from the thundering .44 gouged the wall where the shotgunner had been a heartbeat earlier.

Both survivors were crouched in the two-foot shadow where wall met roof, utterly without cover except for the darkness, undoubtedly very much aware of their unhappy situation but with no place to go but forward.

Bolan swiveled his head but not his eyes as he growled to his flanker, "Spot them?"

"More or less," she replied in a quavery whisper.

"Take them," he said.

He sensed her hesitation and repeated it, more commandingly, "Take them!"

The burper erupted immediately, figure-eighting the left flank and leaping right. The guy with the shotgun jumped up as the burst from the chattergun swept toward him, the weapon at his shoulder in a desperate bid for survival.

The AutoMag roared out a double thunder roll, eclipsing momentarily the chatter from the left. The shotgun blast went toward the moon as the guy was flung back against the wall—and, at that same instant, the fast tattoo from Betsy Gordon's automatic ripped into the guy and held him there for a moment, pinned to the wall, the life forces exploding out of him in a dozen rivers of death.

Bolan went forward to verify the hits. He had to put another round into the first one down. The guy at the center had died on his feet. The one on the left was alive but choking on his own blood.

Betsy had crumpled to one knee, the muzzle of her weapon resting on the cement of the garden patio in the same spot from which she'd been firing.

Bolan trudged back to her position and coldly told her, "Clean it up."

"Wh-what?"

"Your man is suffering. Finish it."

She shrank from that chore.

He lifted her by the arm and guided her to the place. The dying man's eyes were open and pleading as he weakly fought and kept losing to the blood in his throat—the breathing bubbly, lips flecked with red foam.

"Do it!" Bolan commanded.

She could not.

The AutoMag leapt to the task, giving instance to a lingering certainty, then Bolan curled an arm around the girl and led her to the open area beyond the patio wall.

There were no words for the aftermath of this "lesson" in "answers." They waited quietly until Leo Turrin rejoined them.

"On the way," the little guy reported. He was giving the girl a curious inspection. "How far is the lady going?"

"As far as she wants to go," Bolan replied quietly.

"I recommend very, very far," Turrin said. "There's been a slaughter below. The cops are entering the building now."

A question remained unspoken in Betsy's eyes.

Bolan asked it for her. "Any word of another battle?"

The underboss shook his head uncertainly. "I don't know what you mean."

"So there's no word, yet," Bolan said, for the girl's benefit. To Turrin, he explained, "The battle for Quebec. Chebleu is leading a force against the *Mafia Quebeçois*."

"Hell, I hadn't heard of that," Turrin replied.

"You will," Bolan assured him.

Familiar windmill rhythms were approaching through the air from the south.

Turrin said, "Stay hard, Sarge."

"You're not coming?"

The largest little guy shook his head at that. "Wouldn't look right, would it? Naw. I'll wait for the cops in the penthouse." He grinned. "My lawyers will have me sprung from this rap before the cell door closes. Think of all the wild stories I can tell when I get to New York."

Bolan grinned solemnly and clasped the little guy in a bear hug. "Give my best to Hal," he said gruffly.

"Will do. I guess he'll need it. Probably has his tit in a wringer, right now." Eyes flashed to the lady. "Sorry, ma'am."

She'd not even heard. Glistening eyes were on that wall back there.

The chopper was settling in.

The three strolled casually to the touchdown spot. Handshakes all around, a word to the pilot from Leo Turrin, then the little guy was out and clear and the chopper was lifting away from the Tree of Montreal.

The girl collapsed entirely into Bolan's embrace, nuzzling the cold little face onto his shoulder.

She moved moist lips to his ear and whispered, "It's a nightmare."

Sure, Bolan thought, relaxing into his own weary soul. An eternal nightmare.

But also, it was *war*.

EPILOGUE

The helicopter set them down within a two-minute jog of the warwagon. They lost no time claiming the battle cruiser and quitting that area.

Bolan was in bluejeans and flannel shirt, the battered fishing hat, all weapons stowed.

Betsy wore one of Bolan's shirts and nothing else but the effect was little different than that of a mini.

He activated the radio scans and set course for Bois des Filion.

Betsy was awed by the warwagon but as interested in the living accommodations as in the warfare capabilities.

She perched on the seat at Bolan's side and listened to the swirl of intelligence coming through the radio monitors. She had snapped back quickly from that horror on the roof. The color was back in her cheeks and those lovely eyes were finding their proper depths again.

She asked, "Where are we going?"

He told her, "I'm headed to the next combat zone. How about you?"

She showed him a self-conscious smile. "Thanks, no. I think there must be a better way. For me."

He assured her that there was, then said, "I guess I'll stay north of the border until the fur settles a bit. Couple of days in the woods, maybe. A little fishing, a lot of sleeping."

She smiled at that. "A little hunting?"

He rolled his eyes as he replied, "No way. What are your plans? Immediate plans, I mean."

The girl turned up her palms and inspected them. "Gosh, I don't know. I suppose I should try to get back to Andre."

"You can forget that," Bolan told her, lapsing back to the sober mood. "There will be no revolution in Quebec."

She replied, small-voiced, "I know that."

"You knew about Andre—his many lives?"

She nodded. "I knew that he was acting doubly. I guess I've always known that he would one day make the choice one way or the other. I kept hoping it would be *our* way." She spread her hands and tried on a bright smile. "Actually, I guess, every way is our way. Some ways just take longer."

"And last longer," Bolan added.

"Right, right—I guess you're right."

"Want to go fishing with me?"

She giggled, the kid forever. "Sure. Why not?"

Bolan reached over to squeeze her arm and said, "Welcome aboard."

"You, uh, mentioned something else on the program, other than fishing."

"I did?"

"You, uh, said . . . a little fishing, and . . ."

He gave her a sidewise glance and said, "Questions, questions."

She giggled. Hell, he liked that giggle.

"I'll bet you have an answer for that, too," she told him.

"I have *my* answer," he said, smiling.

"I'll settle for that," the ex-guerilla softly told him.

So would Bolan. For a while.

But there were many other questions prowling the landscapes of humanity, savage questions, and the Executioner knew the answers.

A little fishing, a lot of *life* with a grown-up kid who had a lot of that to share, then back to the wars.

Mack Bolan could live with his answers, and it therefore mattered not a damn that he would one day *die* with them.

Could any man ask for any more?

the Executioner

**The gutsiest, most exciting hero in years.
Imagine a guy at war with the Godfather
and all his Mafioso relatives! He's rough,
he's deadly, he's a law unto himself —
nothing and nobody stops him!**

THE EXECUTIONER SERIES by DON PENDLETON

Order		Title	Book #	Price
———	# 1	WAR AGAINST THE MAFIA	P401	$1.25
———	# 2	DEATH SQUAD	P402	$1.25
———	# 3	BATTLE MASK	P403	$1.25
———	# 4	MIAMI MASSACRE	P404	$1.25
———	# 5	CONTINENTAL CONTRACT	P405	$1.25
———	# 6	ASSAULT ON SOHO	P406	$1.25
———	# 7	NIGHTMARE IN NEW YORK	P407	$1.25
———	# 8	CHICAGO WIPEOUT	P408	$1.25
———	# 9	VEGAS VENDETTA	P409	$1.25
———	#10	CARIBBEAN KILL	P410	$1.25
———	#11	CALIFORNIA HIT	P411	$1.25
———	#12	BOSTON BLITZ	P412	$1.25
———	#13	WASHINGTON I.O.U.	P413	$1.25
———	#14	SAN DIEGO SIEGE	P414	$1.25
———	#15	PANIC IN PHILLY	P415	$1.25
———	#16	SICILIAN SLAUGHTER	P552	$1.25
———	#17	JERSEY GUNS	P328	$1.25
———	#18	TEXAS STORM	P353	$1.25
———	#19	DETROIT DEATHWATCH	P419	$1.25
———	#20	NEW ORLEANS KNOCKOUT	P475	$1.25
———	#21	FIREBASE SEATTLE	P499	$1.25
———	#22	HAWAIIAN HELLGROUND	P625	$1.25
———	#23	ST. LOUIS SHOWDOWN	P687	$1.25

TO ORDER

Please check the space next to the book/s you want, send this order form
together with your check or money order, include the price of the book/s
and 25¢ for handling and mailing, to:

PINNACLE BOOKS, INC. / P.O. Box 4347
Grand Central Station/New York, N.Y. 10017

☐ **CHECK HERE IF YOU WANT A FREE CATALOG.**

I have enclosed $_____check_____or money order_____as payment
in full. No C.O.D.'s.

Name_____

Address_____

City_____State_____Zip_____
(Please allow time for delivery.)